Thomas Brisbane

The Early Years of Alexander Smith

Poet and essayist; a study for young men. Chiefly reminiscences of ten years'

companionship

Thomas Brisbane

The Early Years of Alexander Smith
Poet and essayist; a study for young men. Chiefly reminiscences of ten years' companionship

ISBN/EAN: 9783337422868

Printed in Europe, USA, Canada, Australia, Japan

Cover: Foto ©Raphael Reischuk / pixelio.de

More available books at **www.hansebooks.com**

THE EARLY YEARS

OF

ALEXANDER SMITH,

POET AND ESSAYIST.

A Study for Young Men.

CHIEFLY REMINISCENCES OF TEN YEARS' COMPANIONSHIP.

BY THE

REV. T. BRISBANE.

London:

HODDER & STOUGHTON,

27, PATERNOSTER ROW.

M DCCC LXIX.

" We can remember when we knew only the outer childish rim,
and from the crescent guessed the sphere."—*Dreamthorp*.

PREFACE.

VARIOUS sketches of Alexander Smith have already been published since his death. These, however, have been only the brief reminiscences of loving friends of his later years. They may be said to commence with his career of authorship. Their writers seem to have known little of his earlier years of education, aspiration, struggle, and preparatory toil. The information they give of this, the most interesting, instructive, and exemplary period of his life, consists of little more than the date and place of his birth, and the trade to which he served apprenticeship. What has thus been published was indeed worthy of being so; but what has been left untold is none the less worthy of being recorded. His youth was as pure and noble as his manhood. No part of it now demands concealment by the hand of charity. There is consequently a very general regret among his earliest acquaintances and friends that a fuller account of those days has not been written : and several of them, because I was then for several years most closely associated with him in friendship, and so had ample means of knowing " his stream of life from fount to sea," having frequently urged upon me to write such an account, I, at length, so far complied as to give, in the columns of a weekly local journal, a short narrative to its limited number of readers. This, however, so far from satisfying seemed to increase the desire it was designed to gratify; and, consequently, further pressed both by old and several new friends who happened to read that partial account, and whose judgment I cannot but respect, I have ventured to lay this fuller volume before the general public. If I have done so too hastily, it may, perhaps, be deemed pardonable in his earliest friend to have been easily induced to place, though last, some tangible tribute of affectionate remembrance on a grave where so many have already, in one form or other, laid theirs.

The only requisite I possess for the task I have undertaken, is a fuller knowledge of Mr. Smith's early years than others may have. This advantage, however, is counterbalanced by a fear lest my unpractised pen may, after all, fail justly to present the well-known features of so fair a life before the reader's view. Still I cling to the hope that, with a hand moved by affection and steadied and restrained by truth, the work may be so done that the limner and his art may be forgotten, and the face growing before him on these pages, alone command the attention of the reader,—or at least so command it, that he and the critic shall find it easy to exercise charity sufficient to cover any multitude of literary sins which a tyro in book-making may commit.

I aim not at praising the dead; and should I seem to praise, it is because praise I must, where true portraiture itself is praise.

As to method, I follow the example of those

who have preceded me ; by giving chiefly reminiscences of that period of the poet's life best known to me. Doing so will indeed necessitate, however, the employment of the *ego* to an extent which—while I trust neither fulsome nor offensive to the generous reader—I would certainly have preferred to avoid, could I otherwise have told the story as well. After all, it may be better thus; it is only now that reminiscences can well be given ; and by this method, which others have initiated, materials may best be furnished for a competent biographer .in the future. So, poor and faulty as the work may be—

> " I go to plant it on his tomb
> That, if it can, it there may bloom ;
> Or dying, there at least may die."

CONTENTS.

CHAPTER IV.

THE HIGHLANDS.

CHAPTER V.

REVELATIONS.

CHAPTER VI.

THE HIGHLANDS, LOVE, AND ASPIRATIONS.

CHAPTER VII.

THE BARD AND HIS HERALD.

CHAPTER VIII.

"A LIFE DRAMA:" ITS CRITICS, THE PUBLIC, AND POET.

CHAPTER IX.

IN EDINBURGH.

THE EARLY YEARS

OF

ALEXANDER SMITH.

——o——

CHAPTER I.

Birth and Boyhood.

" One whispers here thy boyhood sung
　　Long since its matin song, and heard
　　The low love language of the bird
In native hazels tassel-hung.

The other answers, 'Yea, but here
　　Thy feet have stray'd in after-hours
　　With thy lost friend among the bowers,
And this hath made them trebly dear.'"

TENNYSON.

KILMARNOCK in the county of Ayr, and
　　Paisley in the adjoining county of ·Ren-
frew, have long maintained preëminence among

B

the towns of Scotland in the number of their sons who have been endowed with poetic genius; and Alexander Smith, singularly, had an early connexion with both of these favoured seats of the Scottish muses. In the former he was born, while in the latter he passed his early boyhood and received the first elements of his education.

Being thus a native of the county of Burns, and a nursling of the town of Tannahill and the Wilsons, it may not seem strange that his soul was imbued with a large measure of the poetic spirit. The mantle of endowment which fell upon him, however, was certainly not that of either of these bards. His poetic faculty differed greatly from that of any of these. Burns was intensely Scotch and Tannahill was only a little less so; but in Smith's genius there are no vernacular indications whatever, either in language or sentiment. In expression he is purely English; in spirit broadly cosmopolitan.

His father, Peter Smith, belonged to a village

near Kilmarnock, quaintly called Old Rome, and was by trade a designer—at first of calico printing and afterwards of sewed muslins; while his mother, whose maiden name was Helen Murray—a woman of remarkable mental endowment and tenderest maternal feeling—was a native of the Highlands. In 1829 they took up residence in a humble thatched house situated near the foot of Douglas Street, Kilmarnock; and there on the last day of that year, Alexander, their first child, was born. In one of his productions entitled "A Boy's Poem," which forms part of his "City Poems," he has himself alluded to this fact in representing the "Boy" as saying to his mother—

> "It was the closing evening of the year,
>   The night that I was born. I laughed, and said—
> 'The old year brought me in his dying arms,
>   And laid me in your breast ; his last task done,
>   He went away, through whirls of blinding snow.'"

Both of these his parents still live to mourn the early death of their first-born and gifted son. Between him and his mother there always existed

one of the noblest instances of reciprocal affection
that has ever been manifested in the family circle.
In speaking of her on one occasion in his seventeenth year, with great tenderness of emotion, he
related that he had recently discovered as a fact in
his own history, what he represents the "Boy's"
mother, in the poem already quoted, saying in
answer to her son's reference to the night of his
birth :—

> " 'Tis sixteen years,
> And every night I've looked upon your sleep,
> Although you knew it not."

To be first in maternal affection especially,
seems to be one of the special blessings of primo-
geniture, and this birthright Alexander Smith
always possessed ; and while partiality towards a
first-born has not unfrequently spoiled its object,
it certainly did not do so in his case. He ever
remained worthy of the affection bestowed upon
him, and never did that love receive a better
return than from him. He exhibited in youth
that unyielding truthfulness which he has so highly

extolled in "Alfred Hagart's Household;" while
his gentleness, yet firmness of disposition and
purity of conduct were such as to constrain affection, which he ever answered with more than
ordinary filial devotion towards her who gave it.
His mother may earlier than others have perceived his remarkable genius, and esteemed him
the more on that account; but whether she did
or not, the character of his opening manhood in
a great city was such as could not but win a good
mother's heart, while his unbounded reverence
for her, on the other hand, was doubtless promo-
tive in no small measure of manly virtue. Indeed,
it always seemed to me that this reciprocal affection, which I have seldom seen equalled, and
never seen surpassed, was the real sunshine of
his youth, and therefore demands special notice
in tracing and recording the course of his life.

Shortly after the passing of the Reform Bill in
1832, and so while Alexander was only merging
into boyhood, the trade of Kilmarnock fell into
such a languishing state that Peter Smith, like

many others, was compelled to seek a livelihood elsewhere. And having at length secured a situation in Paisley, he removed with his family to that town in 1834, where they remained for several years, with a brief interval during which, from the vicissitudes of trade, they seem to have been forced back again to Kilmarnock. But they remained for only a brief period in that town on this occasion. Once more they left it, and now finally, by returning to Paisley.

This early removal from Kilmarnock, may be regarded as the reason of no particular reference being found in his works to that town or its environs. No poet or literary man has drawn more largely—it might, perhaps, be said so largely —from his own life, history, and experience, or confined his descriptions more to scenes familiarised to him by actual residence, than Alexander Smith. You seldom find him far from home in his works. None of his readers require to be told where he has lived, except in this one instance. Kilmarnock is unquestionably the Spiggleton of

"Alfred Hagart's Household," but it is not described in the novel as Greysley and Hawkhead are. In fact there are only a few incidental allusions in one of his latest works—"A Summer in Skye"—to indicate that he had ever been in Ayrshire. It sufficiently accounts for this that, he left Kilmarnock at too infantine an age for that town and its neighbourhood to have made any distinct and lasting impressions on his imagination and memory. The poet's eye had not yet opened within him, and Ayrshire remained almost a *terra incognita* till near the end of his short life. It was in Paisley that his being opened to a perception of the beauties of nature and the charms of literature. In this town—which he has compared to "an aviary of singing birds," called "the abode of poetic inspiration," and described so graphically towards the close of the second volume of "A Summer in Skye," and also under the name of Greysley in "Alfred Hagart's Household"—he spent his early boyhood, and acquired the elements of the art of reading. As far as school learning is concerned,

that is nearly all that can be said regarding his
education in Paisley. Partly owing to his residence in that town also being only of short dura-
tion, and from other causes immediately to be referred to, his school attainments were of the most
rudimentary character when the family again
removed. At the time of that removal he was too
young to have read the writings of Tannahill,
Motherwell, Alex. Wilson, and John Wilson—
better known as Christopher North,—or the numerous less illustrious poets of that remarkably
poetic town ; and also too young to have become
acquainted with, and been capable of appreciating,
the scenery made classic by their walks, musings,
and poems. The only part of the scenery around
Paisley which had been painted in unfading poetic
colouring on his youthful mind, was that stretching
for two or three miles along the course of the
Glasgow and Paisley Canal, near to which he
resided ; and the impressions which he then received of that locality he has faithfully and
felicitously expressed in " Alfred Hagart's House-

hold." It was during a short sojourn, in after years, at the neighbouring village of Williamsburgh, that he began to ramble among

" Gleniffer's bonny woods and braes."

It would certainly be wrong to say that the last mentioned work, or, indeed, that any of Mr. Smith's works, is autobiographical; yet in several of them, and especially in it, there is a great deal of the author's personal history, contemplated under a poetic atmosphere, wrought up, as no one even slightly acquainted with him and his family can fail to perceive. The original of almost every character in that novel is easily enough discoverable within the circle of his relatives and friends. In some instances, indeed, the likeness is closer than is commendable in fictitious writing; but there is one character in that tale, the delineation of which could not offend the sensitiveness of any one, while it must charm every reader, and for the execution of which the writer deserves highest praise. It is that of little " Katy Hagart."

In sketching that character Mr. Smith was indulging one of the most hallowed recollections of his early days in Paisley, and of an event which he was often wont to refer to, but never without deep emotion. It was to him especially, but also to all connected with him, an ever sadly memorable event. It happened that he fell dangerously ill of fever when a boy, and for a short time his life was despaired of. At length, however, he slowly recovered, though at the cost of being slightly marred in appearance for life, as, through weakening or contraction of the nerves of one eye under the power of the disease, it retained ever after a squint. In times of vigorous health this defect, though visible, was not great; but on occasion of any temporary indisposition, it became invariably increased, and so gave indication to his friends of his state of health. His constitution was also for a number of years, in fact, until he became publicly known, enfeebled by this fever. He was rendered peculiarly liable to take cold, which always induced a short, unpleasant, barking cough—a yearly complaint, which caused him and his family frequent concern. But worse than this befell :—

> " While yet a child
> He had a playmate in his summer sports,—
> Inseparable they were as sun and shade "—

a sister, some two years or so younger than himself, who was also stricken down by the fever, and who died of it before he had fully recovered, so that he saw her no more, and

> " For years his heart was darkened like a grave
> By a sepulchral yew."

Her death made a very deep and solemn impression upon his young spirit, and awakened within him his religious instincts, and also his poetic faculties. The memory of her fair young form, and life, and early death, remained fresh through after-years on his sensitive heart, and became ever increasingly surrounded with a glowing atmosphere of poetic radiance. Her death refined and enriched his being. It was to him so far gain. She became to him henceforth a companion angel—an unseen spiritual presence always near him. While still quite a young lad, therefore, he read often, with much melancholy fondness and tender emotion, Leigh Hunt's essay on "Deaths of Little Children," and Longfellow's "Footsteps of Angels." I have frequently heard him, with his wondrously impressive intonation of voice, quote especially the following words of Hunt—"Death arrested her with his kindly harshness, and blessed her into an eternal image of youth and innocence."

But another important incident connected with his education happened during his convalescence at this time. He had never as yet read a book through, but his mother one day put into his still feeble hands "Bunyan's Pilgrim's Progress," which entirely captivated his mind, excited his imagination, and sent his thoughts wandering through dream-land to an extent which must rather have retarded than promoted his recovery to perfect health. The reader of "A Boy's Poem" will find

there a reference to this fact of his history also, in
the passage beginning—

> "In those dark days I was surprised with joy—
> The deepest I have found upon the earth.
> One night, when my weak limbs were drawing strength
> From meats and drinks, and long delicious sleep,
> I raised a book to kill the tedious hours—
> The glorious dreamer's," etc.

These two incidents made him at once poetical in
feeling and imaginative thought. The Highland
servant girl too of "Alfred Hagart's Household,"
is not altogether a myth. The original of that
character I have several times heard him speak
of as either domesticated, or at least a frequent
visitor, at his own home in Paisley, and her weird
stories had also a considerable influence in stimu-
lating his naturally poetic mind. But while he was
thus under the power of these three teachers—
death, Bunyan, and the narrator of Ossianic
legends—the boy was removed from Paisley to
Glasgow.

After the family had settled in Glasgow,

Alexander was sent to prosecute his education at a school in John Street, which was conducted by Mr. Niel Livingstone, who ultimately became a minister of the Free Church of Scotland, and still labours with acceptance as pastor of the church connected with that denomination in the parish of Stair in Ayrshire. His love of learning, the readiness with which he acquired it, together with his seriousness of spirit and thoughtfulness of disposition, induced his parents to entertain the desire of educating him for the Christian ministry in connexion with the Secession Church; and at this time that was deemed by himself the most desirable of all occupations. The necessities of the family, however, required that he should soon begin to do something towards his own support: and consequently, though the purpose was not at once wholly abandoned, he meantime left school, when he had received only a meagre education, being an entire stranger to the classics, only very partially acquainted with English grammar, and poorly versed in geography; in short, he could read well, write well, and cast up ordinary accounts tolerably well. That was the whole amount of his school education.* Mr. Smith,

---

* It is true that another account has been given of this matter. In *Good Words* of March 1867, appeared the following : " It is common to speak of such men who have not had the advantage of a University training, as more or less wonderful samples of self education, and Smith has in this way been described as 'self-taught.' In the sense of which it is true of every man of any force and originality, he was self-taught. But it would be a great mistake to forget that he had received the benefit of that wise provision which Scotland has for centuries made for the education of her children. Smith's early education embraced a good know-ledge of English, arithmetic, and geography ; some history and the elements of mathematics and Latin. A youth so furnished with the capacity and will to carry on his education by the study of the best works in literature, need not, perhaps, form any subject of condescending wonder, when it is found that he can write good poetry and prose, and even prove himself in the kingdom of letters the peer of professors and senior wranglers." But there is a very palpable vein of exaggeration running through the whole passage regarding Smith's early advantages, from which this extract is taken. That "his *early* education embraced a *good* knowledge " of all the above branches is not correct. I speak what I know, and confidently affirm that, if ever he acquired a good knowledge, or any knowledge, of mathematics, it was after he went to Edin-burgh as secretary of the University. Certainly mathematics

therefore, was not only a truly self-taught man, but he was so with merely the very ordinary school education usually given to a working man's son thirty years ago, to begin with. To state the plain truth in this matter is only to ascribe the more, and the due amount of honour to his memory, while it renders the lesson of his life all the more encouraging and stimulative to the youth of that class to which he belonged. Thus equipped then, when he was under twelve years of age—a period of life when it really was not possible to have acquired all the branches of education ascribed to him by some—the event happened which he has expressed in the following lines—

> "So on a summer morning I was led
> Into a square of warehouses, and left
> 'Mong faces merciless as engine wheels."

His object now was to learn his father's occupation,

---

never formed any part of his *early* education, nor did a good knowledge of the elements of Latin ; for what he did learn of the rudiments of that language was under my tuition, several years after he had left school.

which at that time was a lucrative one to at least a few talented individuals. He had formed no companionships previously at school, nor, while always frank and social with those near his own age among whom he toiled, did he form any real companionship among them for two or three years; so that in the great city,

> "' Mid the eternal hum, the boy clomb up
> Into a shy and solitary youth,
> With strange joys and strange sorrows."

He had already read much for his years, and his mornings and evenings were still devoted to reading. "Books were his chiefest friends." The works of the English poets, particularly of Byron and Wordsworth, at this time delighted him most, for he had not yet formed acquaintance with Shelley, Keats, and Tennyson, who afterwards became his chief teachers. Next to poetry, he was addicted to the reading of history, travels, and novels. In novel reading, however, his natural literary taste made him eclectic. From his earliest days, Scott was his favourite in this department of literature,

C

and after Scott came Cooper. Several of the American tales of the latter, which he read at a very early age, made a deep impression on his imagination, and constrained him to seek fuller knowledge of the scenery, history, and literature of that country. Among the first books of travels which he consequently read was Stephens' travels in South America ; and it, together with Cooper's novels, so excited his mind, that the first poem of any length which he composed was an American tale of love and war, entitled " Black Eagle," from the name of the hero of the piece, who was an Indian warrior. This poem was written rapidly about his sixteenth year, but was soon afterwards destroyed, being judged by his ripening genius unworthy of preservation. But it was by no means his first poetic effort. From earliest boyhood " his own heart made him a poet," and in school days he often indulged in writing verses.

The warehouse in which he was first employed was that of Alexander Buchanan & Co., on the right hand of Queen Court, Queen Street. His occupation here consisted in tracing the lines of sewed muslin designs with lithographic ink ; and as this process of "penning," as it is technically called, is wholly mechanical, though the first step towards designing, his mind had freedom to pursue its poetic fancies. It was, therefore, so far, an advantageous occupation for him, and he prized it on that account. The muses were with him all day at his work, and he encouraged and gave attentive ear to their whisperings. The piece of paper used under the hand of the penner, to prevent contact with the prepared surface of the design, was often by night filled with hasty scribblings, and was then rolled up and deposited in his vest pocket. These scribblings were polished and expanded at home before the young poet retired to bed, or in the still hours of early morning.

> "Oft a fine thought would flush his face divine,
> As he had quaffed a cup of golden wine
> Which deifies the drinker : oft his face
> Gleamed like a spirit's in that shady place,
> While he saw smiling upward from the scroll
> The image of the thought within his soul."

Then, moved by boyish ecstatic impulse, he would leap from his seat, seize its cushion in both hands, and bring it down with a sudden thwack upon the shoulders of his unsuspecting youthful neighbour, when a brief frolicsome encounter ensued. For these raptures, and other little eccentricities, his shopmates playfully dubbed him with the title of "Daft Sandie." He was at this time a long-limbed lad, with large unfilled bones, rather ungainly in appearance and careless in dress; sallow in complexion, and of a somewhat sad expression of countenance, from precocious thoughtfulness, and of a diffident disposition. In the evening he might be seen walking homewards alone, the thumb of each hand generally thrust into his vest pocket, his head stooping forward till it nearly rested on his breast, and trudging with heavy gait and long strides like one accustomed too early to plod over soft ploughed land. His appearance then was, consequently, very unlike what it became in after years, and especially as he neared middle life, and indeed was by no means prepossessing.

It was at this time, however, when about thirteen or fourteen years of age, that he first felt the tender passion of love, an event to which he refers in the following lines—

> " Love oped the dusty volume of my life,
>   And wrote, with his own hot and hurrying hand,
>   A chapter in fierce splendours.   Then it was
>   I built an altar, raised a flame to love,
>   And a strong whirlwind blew the altar down,
>   And strewed its sparks in darkness."

The object of this his first and boyish affection, was a tall and graceful dark-haired and dark-eyed maiden, several years his senior to appearance, who was employed in the same warehouse, and whom he has celebrated in " A Boy's Poem," and also refers to in " A Life Drama " thus—

> " One, a queenly maiden fair,
>   Sweepeth past me with an air :
>   Kings might kneel beneath her stare ;
>   Round her heart, a rose-bud free,
>   Reeled I, like a drunken bee,
>   Alas ! it would not ope to me."

His affection for this damsel was a transitory one.

He was speedily cured of it by discovering that she
was affianced to another warehouse lad of maturer
age, and henceforth she became only one of the
"fair shapes which pace the garden of his memory."
It was merely for poetic uses, and not because of
any serious wound inflicted on his heart, that he
cherished a fond remembrance of her in after years.
I have a vivid recollection of seeing him almost
daily about this time ; but it was some two years
after, when he was designer in another house, that
I became personally acquainted with him. When,
towards the close of 1846, our friendship really
commenced, he was employed in Messrs. John
Robertson & Sons', at the corner of Exchange
Square, Queen Street, near

> " Where merchants congregate,
> And where the mighty war-horse snorts in bronze."

He has himself introduced his readers into the
scene of his daily toils at this time, and favoured
them with an imaginary conversation conducted by
his fellow-workers, in the passage beginning at
page 8 of " City Poems." Some of those among

whom he wrought were young men of more than ordinary talent and culture. The verses of one occasionally graced the poet's corner of the city newspapers; another wrote and published a drama, the scene of which was laid in the Noachian age; while a third was a painter in water colours of very considerable ability. They all, however, regarded Sandie—as they familiarly named him—as their superior in genius and literary attainments though he was the youngest of all.

One of the chief excellencies of Smith's genius consists in his graphic portraiture of persons, and curt but clear delineation of character. Few poets have equalled him in sketching off a character in one short sentence. His first efforts at full length portraiture were not very successful, but his power in this grew, and still was growing rapidly when he died. The character of Bertha in "Edwin of Deira" is well sustained, and far surpasses anything of the same kind which he had previously done; but even that is excelled by his after effort in the character of Miss Catherine Macquarrie in "Alfred

Hagart's Household." That is a most symmetrical, natural, and noble character. It astonished all his friends, and its execution must have been contemplated by himself with much laudable pride; for he was early sensible of his ability of accomplishment falling short of his ambition in dramatic delineation. In miniature painting, however, he was an adept from his youth. His earliest works abound with inimitable miniatures, and he has seldom manifested this talent more happily than in describing his shopmates. Thus :--

> " He at my right hand ever dwelt alone ;
>   A moat of dulness fenced him from the world.
>   My left-hand neighbour was all flame and air—
>   A restless spirit, veering like the wind ;
>   And what a lover ! what an amorous heart !
>   In the pure fire and fervency of love,
>   Leander, like the image of a star
>   Within the thrilling sea, was scarce his match.
>   His love for each new hero of a week
>   No Hellespont could cool.   Among the rest
>   Sat one with visage red with sun and wind,
>   As the last hip upon the frosted brier,
>   When the blithe huntsman snuffs the hoary morn.

    *   *   *   *   *

> " And there was one
> Who strove most valiantly to be a man ;
> Who smoked, and still got sick, drank hard, and woke
> Each morn with headache ; his poor timorous voice
> Trembled beneath the burden of the oaths
> His bold heart made it bear.
>
> * * * * *
>
> " Harry's laughing face
> Filled with his mischievous and merry eyes."

These are all true life-pictures which his early friends cannot fail to identify.

Mr. Smith gave good promise of excelling in the profession of designer, had he fully devoted himself to it, but he never did so. He could not regard it as the profession of his life. His heart was too strongly inclined towards literature and poetry, and, consequently, he did not rise to the first rank as a designer. Very soon after entering a ware-house he ceased also to entertain the desire and prospect of becoming a preacher of the gospel. His own reasons for this shall be given anon in his own words. For several years he had, therefore, no definite purpose of life-work before him. His growing ambition was to be a true poet, but he was, at the same time, convinced that some other occupation required to be pursued in order to gain a steady livelihood—hence the dictum—

"The lunatic, the lover, and the poet,
Are of imagination all compact,"

was not verified in his case. Meantime he was content to toil on and wait his day, doing all the while his best to serve his employers during ware-house hours ; and the fact that he was retained in the service of Messrs. Robertson for six or seven years, and then left it and the trade of designer simultaneously, and of his own accord, proves that he was a faithful and valued workman. During all these years of industrious toil, he was morning and night educating himself by reading, and cultivating his poetic talent by writing. He had become a most voluminous reader of all kinds of literature. His most intimate friends wondered how, with so little time at his command, he could amass such a knowledge of books as he possessed. He was endowed, however, with a most tenacious and ready memory. By his seventeenth year he knew better than most persons almost all the English poets from the times of Chaucer. But Keats and Tennyson were now his favourites.

It was his custom about this time, to confine his reading and study for a period principally to one author, till he had mastered him, and then devote himself similarly to another. Thus, for a considerable time, he read all he could lay his hands on of the works of Byron, with critiques on these, or whatever had been written by others relating to the life and writings of that extraordinary genius. Shelley next for a while engaged his leisure hours; then Coleridge, or Wordsworth, or Keats, Tennyson, Campbell, Thomson, Burns, Shakespeare, Spenser, Chaucer, had each a season of study given specially to him. And one of less wide fame than either of these, who became for a time a very great favourite, must not be forgot—Ebenezer Elliott, the Corn Law rhymer. His reading in other departments of literature, however, was of the most desultory and fortuitous nature. He had then a great partiality for editions of the poets in small volumes, seemingly because he could carry them in his pocket to read in his rambles, or consult and refresh his memory with at any spare moment. Indeed, he was never to be found without some favourite book on his person.

CHAPTER II.

The Addisonian Society.

" Where once we held debate, a band
Of youthful friends, on mind and art,
And labour, and the changing mart,
And all the framework of the land."

TENNYSON.

IN the year 1846, a few young men, nearly all of whom were employed in warehouses formed themselves into a Literary Society for essay-writing and debate. This club met every Saturday evening; and after it had been a few weeks in existence, Smith was introduced to its membership by "bright-eyed Harry," and I thus became more fully acquainted with him than I had been previously. Of this society he was, for the following seven years, a regular attender and the greatest ornament. Each member was necessitated by the rules to read in rotation an essay of his own composition, and it soon came to his turn to occupy the desk. The subject of his prelections I have forgot; but I have a vivid recollection of the introduction, and also of the general impression made by the whole upon the members. The introduction was an elaborated picture, glowing with rich colouring, of Old Father Time sitting meditatively among the ruins of an old feudal pile by moonlight, with the roll of earth's history, partly unfolded, in his hand. The essay from its beginning took the members by surprise, and they listened unto the close with fixed silence and increasing admiration. When the essayist sat down, no one felt disposed to speak. Criticism was disarmed. At length only the most fervent eulogies were expressed. The appearing of "A Life Drama" did not make a more profound sensation on the public than the reading of his first essay did on the society that night. He had been previously almost silent as a member, but they had now discovered his ability, and he was tacitly by all placed first in membership. He gave a great stimulus to the club. Till then the debates seemed generally most interesting, and the society was in danger of becoming an arena of wranglers ; but from that night the debates were doomed to a second place. The ablest members' hearts were made to glow with unwonted warmth in laudable emulation, and the writing of essays became henceforth a serious, earnest, and arduous affair. After one or two abortive attempts, several, made conscious of being too far distanced, withdrew from membership ; but their places were soon filled by others of superior ability. The society continued to be characterised by great enthusiasm till the end of winter, and the most literary of the members having found it a most genial and profitable scene of intercourse, proposed to continue in session during the summer months also ; but the less aspiring objected to this, and proposed an adjournment till the beginning of next winter, and these carried the vote. Smith and other three agreed among themselves, however, to meet every alternate Saturday evening in a coffee-house. There a few others joined them during the summer, and by the commencement of the following winter, there were about twenty regular attenders. This club was now designated "The Addisonian Literary Society." Its regular place of meeting, during the greater part of its history, was in Mons. Simeon's class-room, at the corner of Frederick Street, in George Square. It was among the *élite* of its members that Smith found his inmost and almost sole circle of friendship, till he was brought into public notice by the Rev. Geo. Gilfillan. And although none of them possessed equal genius, or were so extensively read in general literature as he, several of them were young men of sufficient culture and mental endowment to constitute them not only worthy friends of his youth, but also acquaintances by whose intercourse he might and did profit. One, for example, though employed as an engraver, and having no thought of aspiring to literary fame, possessed a tropical exuberance of imagination, which Smith ever admired, and which even surpassed his own, although it was less chaste and restrained. His essays were burdened with imagery, often, indeed, of the wildest, but always of the most original kind. Even his common conversation sparkled with metaphoric gems. The " Life Drama" is indebted to him for some of its many fine figures. I have a lively remembrance of sitting with him and Smith one night reading, with many pauses and interlacings of racy comment, and no little wild laughter, Gilfillan's " Bards of the Bible," as it came fresh from the press. Other two members of the club were students in the University, who now occupy pulpits of different denominations. Another was a diligent student of physical science, who while occupying one of the very humblest posts of unskilled labour, was well known in the centre of the city as "the man with the book," from never being seen on even its busiest streets but threading his way with eyes fixed on the open pages of some volume; and thus fitted himself for reading papers with credit before the Geological Society

D

of Glasgow, of which he was an honoured member, and, finally, by plodding mental industry rose to secure a place on the staff of the Government Survey.

And there was one of most versatile genius and unbounded wit and comicality—"a fellow of infinite jest"—who unfortunately, failed to fulfill the promise of his youth, and when last heard of by his early friends, by means of a letter he addressed from America to Smith in Edinburgh, described himself as having lived a curiously chequered life in the New World;—at one time sailing with the bargemen on the Mississippi; anon starring on the stage; next smoking with members of Congress; then bivouacking with wandering gipsies; soon after drinking champagne with the President of the States; and finally, having undertaken the editorship of an influential newspaper, solicited his old fellow-Addisonian, now secretary of Edinburgh University, to become his correspondent for Scotland. Another, a voracious reader and devoted student of natural philosophy, possessed two faculties in a degree that I have never known equalled in any other person—retentiveness of memory, and the sense of poetic taste. The latter faculty he seemed to possess with the quickness and keenness of an exquisite sense of touch, while his memory was so tenacious that I have heard him, shortly after having read two pages of poetry only once, repeat the whole almost perfectly. His essays were models of graceful diction. His powers of original thought and of ratiocination, however, were not equally great. The stores of other men, which lay in his mind, appeared to induce personal inactivity, and prevent the invigorating exercise of his own powers of cogitation; for he often played the part of the plagiarist. He was withal a most eccentric genius, wearing at midsummer a top coat, close buttoned to the chin, and carrying a small copy of Shelley's poems in the breast pocket; having his shirt collar rolled over in the style of Byron; then changing it for a season after the manner of Keats, his next favourite bard.

Slender in form and solitary in life, no one
knew his relations, and he was never heard to
speak of them. He seemed to have no senior
friends. He was alone in the great city, ever
copying the ways of men of literary eminence.
Having read, as he said, of Dr. Johnson drinking
sixteen cups of tea at a sitting; he without ascer-
taining the size of the cup, would, to the annoyance of his landlady, try to do so also, and so
injured his stomach that he was confined to his
room for two or three days. At length he became
a Unitarian preacher, and went to England, taking
with him a wife who doubtless soon cured him
of his vagaries, and set reasonable limits to his
tea drinking. Smith was wont to show great
deference to his literary taste and judgment, and
honoured him among the first to whom he
privately submitted his poetry, and as one of the
very few whom he confidentially consulted regarding sending his MS., to the Rev. George Gilfillan.
It was to this member of the club also that Smith
was first and chiefly indebted for his knowledge of

the names of our Scottish wild flowers, and the
little acquaintance with botany which he acquired;
and together with him he also received, for a
short time, from another Addisonian, lessons in
the rudiments of the Latin language; but neither
of the two ever prosecuted that study to any profitable extent. Smith visited this early friend
and spent a day with him, on the occasion of his
first trip to England after the publication of " A
Life Drama." He may be regarded as the Wat
of " Horton "—

> " Poor Wat ! once proud as chanticleer that struts
>   Among his dames ; faint challenged, claps his wings
>   And crows defiance to the distant farms—
>   Now meekly sits beneath a shrewish voice,
>   With children round his knee."

Till his death Smith retained a tender regard
for him and the other members of the Addisonian
Society.

The last time I had the pleasure of seeing him
in Edinburgh, after inquiring, as he never failed
to do, regarding several of them, he said,—" Well,

that society did us both a vast amount of good ; for myself, I know I derived much benefit from it. Through its means I was first stimulated to composition, and had my latent powers roused to action." When it was his night to read an essay there was always a full meeting of the members, and as each had the liberty of bringing a friend with him, there were generally a few strangers also present. Never but once, as far as I remember, did he fail on these occasions to produce a carefully thought out and well composed paper. The minute book of the society, which is still carefully preserved by its last secretary, shows the following to be the subjects on which he wrote: "Intellect," "on Man," "the claims of History on Man," "on Religious Poetry," "Earnestness," "on Progress," "Addison," characterised in the minutes as "beautiful remarks" on that writer ; "Thoughts anent Life," commended for its composition, but condemned by the members for the gloomy and desponding view the essayist took of our present state of civilisation ; "Thoughts on Napoleon,"

"Thoughts on a Friend," "John Keats," "Ebenezer Elliott," "Burns as a National Poet." This, his last essay in the society, was read on November 13, 1852, and was regarded as "not only the best and most finished of all Mr. Smith's productions, but also as the best essay ever read in the society." It appeared almost verbatim shortly afterwards in the short lived *Glasgow Miscellany*, of which Smith was editor; and a considerable amount of it was made available in the exquisite life of Burns, which he prefixed to the edition of that poet's works which he edited in 1865.

The fame which Smith at length suddenly acquired as a poet, by the pages of the *Eclectic* and *Critic* in 1851, and 1852 proved indirectly the chief cause of the death of the Addisonian Society. Although it had now served, for him and his most intimate friends, the purpose for which they had joined it, he still loved it as a place of pleasant intercourse, and desired to remain connected with it; but several of the members now treated him and spoke to him with such un-

wonted tokens of deference, on account of his rising
fame, and made such allusions to his poetry as
galled his manly spirit. They often brought also
young students and silly literary aspirants to the
club, who sat and so stared at the poet that the
place became unendurable, and he consequently
frequently failed to be present. With a few others
he endeavoured to save the society by reconsti-
tuting it from a limited selection of the oldest
members, and changing the place of meeting;
but, after all, a few hilarious students from the
country got in, and so changed the character of
the club that Smith and his chief friends withdrew altogether, and it soon became defunct from
lack of earnestness of purpose and sobriety of
spirit. It had, however, served a good end. There
have been clubs in the city of greater pretensions,
which have had their praises sounded by eminent
men; but it may be questioned if any of them
existed to better purpose than the Addisonian.
It produced Alexander Smith. He himself, on
the day on which it was arranged that he should

appear as a tale-writer in *Good Words*, confessed
his indebtedness to it; and if the public have in
any measure benefited by his writings, they have
indirectly at least profited in part by this club.
Some of the passages and ornaments of his poems,
too, were at least originally suggested to his mind
by intercourse with its members. These two lines,
for example, describing the earth and heavens as

> " A theatre magnificently lit
> For sorry acting, undeserved applause,"

occur in an essay read before the society, and
still preserved by one of the members, who had
no idea he was writing poetry. I have also a vivid
recollection of several times reading a letter
addressed to Mr. Smith by an Addisonian in which
—describing a melancholy drive he had in a gig,
in a gloomy state of mind, from a railway station
in Lanarkshire, on a dark wet night,—the original
of the following graphic passage of " A Boy's
Poem " occurred :—

> " I paused upon a drear bewildered road,
> Lined with dark trees, or ghosts, which only seemed

A darker gloom in gloom, and far away
A glare went up as of a sunken fire.
'This is the land of death, and that is hell.'
I cried, as I went on toward the glare :
I climbed a bank of gloom, and here I saw
A burning sea upon a burning shore—
A lone man sitting black against the light ;
The long black shadow stretching o'er the sands,
Long as earth's sunset shades."

The fine passage too in " A Life Drama," beginning—" My friend, a poet must ere long arise ; " is only the more melodious utterance of the impassioned words of a brother Addisonian, expressed in a colloquy on poets, carried on while a few of us were walking in the western outskirts of the city.

It is true that Smith was not associated or connected in his youth with any of the recognised or distinguished literary men of Glasgow ;* still,

---

* To say as a writer in *Good Words*, March, 1867, has done, in treating of his early education—" Smith had the advantage in Glasgow of intimate intercourse with men of cultivated literary and poetic powers. Among these were the late Professor Nicholl, Mr. J. Hedderwick, and Mr. Hugh Macdonald," is not a little mislead-

as this chapter may serve to show, he was not entirely isolated from genial and profitable society. Indeed, among the members of the Addisonian club, he may have enjoyed society more fitting his own years, educational acquirements, and mental growth, than he would then have done among men of more advanced culture and ripened experience. It is questionable if he would have found among more natured minds, a more inspiring and bracing sphere of self discipline in his earliest years than he did here. By the time he became known to the world, however, he had indeed outgrown all his Glasgow associates. The period had then arrived when the necessities of his genius and whole mental nature, required that he should be severed from these, and mix with men of larger growth as his friends and equals. And it was well for him that, when the ripeness of the occasion came, he so

---

ing; for the truth is, he did not know one of these individuals personally till after George Gilfillan brought him into public notice, as shall be shown in the sequel of this narrative.

readily found hands outstretched to welcome him within the desiderated sphere. His removal to Edinburgh, "residence in which is an education in itself," as he has said, was well-timed, as it was very needful, and proved most advantageous. The truth is, no poet or literary man that has arisen from the ranks of the common people, has been more kindly dealt with in Providence, especially in the first stages of his career, than Alexander Smith.

CHAPTER III.

The Clyde.

" Oh I remember, and will ne'er forget
    Our meeting spots, our chosen sacred hours,
    Our burning words that uttered all the soul,
    Our faces beaming with unearthly loves,
    Sorrow with sorrow sighing, hope with hope
    Exulting, heart embracing heart entire."
                        POLLOCK.

IT has been asserted that Smith, previous to the publication of his first volume of poems, was almost wholly indebted to books for his knowledge of rural scenery, and the fact that he has notwithstanding given many admirable descriptions of such scenery, has been adduced as a proof of his eminent genius. This, however, is a mistake, which has perhaps originated in understanding too literally such lines as—

" For years and years continually were mine—
    The long dull roar of traffic, and at night
    The mighty pathos of the empty streets."

The fact is, there is no attempt made by him in all his works, of describing scenery merely through acquaintance with books, unless it be in the passage of "A Life Drama," beginning—"In the green lanes of Kent," or in the use of such phrases as "Lincoln Fens," and these can scarcely be called descriptions. And in this and subsequent chapters, it will be shown that, by the time he wrote his first book, he had seen and rambled among more of the rich scenery of Scotland than most of his countrymen have ever done.

But, meantime, let us return to 1846, in order to follow another thread of his life story from that date.

A few weeks after Smith's admission into the Addisonian Society, our intercourse commenced, which soon ripened into more than acquaintance-ship. On the evening of the last Saturday in October of that year, while passing along Argyle Street, purposing to get out of the city in quest of solitude, he suddenly accosted me, and proposed a walk previous to the assembling of our club.

And as he had heard of my intention to enter college on the following Monday, we were speedily engaged in conversation on our respective hopes and aims in life. Mine were so far fixed, and interested him ; but his were dim and uncertain. As he then informed me, however, he had till very recently ardently entertained · a similar prospect to that which I was about to prosecute. Our conversation thus become close and confidential, as walking on, we left the city behind us, and journeyed several miles along the Cathcart Road, aided by the light of the Hutchiesontown furnaces. At length we returned to our club, no longer acquaintances but friends, and under a mutual promise to meet again on the afternoon of that day week. That was to me, and I hope in some measure also to him, a fortunate though accidental meeting. I had then no idea of the character and calibre of the youth I had ignorantly endeavoured to shun. The treasure of friendship, and the profit which in various ways I derived for years from that casual meeting, cannot be told nor estimated.

" An opulent soul
Dropt in my path like a great cup of gold,
All rich and rare with stories of the gods."

And now

"It is the proudest memory of my youth
That I was his familiar and beloved."

During the whole of the winter, we spent every Saturday afternoon together, and very rarely was there a third person present. Then as summer drew on, and the college had closed for the session, we met almost every night as he came out of the warehouse. This practice we continued for more than six years. Talking much on many themes, we frequently conversed of personal matters; rehearsed each other's history, forecast our hopes, and told the secrets of the soul, as far as one may to his fellow-mortal, and as one can only do to the closest and sincerest friend in the spring of unsophisticated youth. Each summer evening when the sky was clear, we walked from eight till ten o'clock. Our favourite and most frequent path being "beside the river that we used to love."

> " Beneath the crescent moon on autumn nights,
>   We paced its banks with overflowing hearts,
>   Discoursing long of great thought-wealthy souls,
>   And with what spendthrift hands they scatter wide
>   Their spirit-wealth, making mankind their debtors.
>   *   *   *   *   *
>   Or haply talked of dearer personal themes,
>   Blind guesses at each other's after-fate ;
>   Feeling our leaping hearts, we marvelled oft
>   How they should be unleashed, and have free course
>   To stretch and strain far down the coming time."

And on Saturday, when at an earlier hour than on the other days of the week,

> " Labour laid down his tools and went away—
>   The park was loud with games, clear laughter shrieks
>   Came from the rings of girls around the trees ;
>   The cricketers were eager at their play,
>   The stream was dotted with the swimmers' heads,
>   Gay boats flashed up and down.
>   *   *   *   *
>   We hurried on,
>   Through all the mirth, to where the river ran,
>   In the grey evening, 'tween the hanging woods,"

of sweet Kenmúir, "with a soul-soothing murmur."

Many are the allusions to this wood in " A Life Drama" and the " City Poems." It was our favourite haunt during all these six years. There is no walk around Glasgow equal to that of about six miles, by the windings of the Clyde, to Kenmuir; and during this time we must have enjoyed it at least twenty times each year—on the Saturday afternoons. The wood affords some of the finest glimpses of sylvan and river scenery I have ever seen. With its changing moods, no lover of the beautiful can ever weary of it. The ground, moreover, is thickly carpeted with the richest variety of wild flowers; and here with several of these we formed our first acquaintance. Whole beds of blue hyacinth fill the air with their delicious odour.

> " Oh, fair the wood on summer days,
> While a blue hyacinthine haze
> Is dreaming round the roots!"

There, also, are beds of primrose, violet, cranesbill, speedwell, starwort, woodruff; and it is the only place for many miles around the city where you will find the yellow globe-flower, or "lucken gowan" of the Ettrick Shepherd. This wood is less than a mile above the sweetly picturesque village or "clachan" of Carmyle, where the Clyde flows murmuringly over a crescent-shaped weir, constructed, apparently, to secure a supply of water to two dusty meal mills and other works. For a short distance, both below and above this spot, there is very exquisite wood and water scenery; but Kenmuir Bank is the gem of this part of the Clyde. It is a narrow steep, rising from the river to a height of about 60 or 70 feet, and so closely covered with trees that all summer there is "a green gloaming in the wood," to use one of the happy phrases of Hugh Macdonald, who knew the place well, loved it much, and has honoured it with one of his sketches in his "Rambles Round Glasgow." At the bottom of the bank, towards its east end, there is a perennial spring of peculiarly pleasant water, called the Marriage Well, to which there is the following reference, among others, in "A Life Drama."

Within yon grove of beeches is a well.

*   *   *   *   *

Memories grow around it thick as flowers.

*   *   *   *   *

Beside that well I read the mighty Bard,
Who clad himself with beauty, genius, wealth ;
Then flung himself on his own passion-pyre
And was consumed,"

which is an autobiographic fact. Frequently have we sat together for hours, one on each side of the spring, on long summer evenings, reading aloud by turns the English poets. All Byron's minor poems and greater part of "Childe Harold," several plays of Shakespeare, the poems of Keats, and many others did we thus read "covered with secrecy and silence there." And

" Sometimes we sat whole afternoons, and watched
The sunset build a city frail as dream,
With bridges, streets of splendour, towers; and saw
The fabrics crumble into rosy ruins,
And then grow grey as heath."

" Breezes are blowing in old Chaucer's verse,
'Twas here we drank them ; here for hours we hung
O'er the fine pants and trembles of a line.
Oft, standing on a hill's green head, we felt

> Breezes of love, and joy, and melody,
> Blow through us, as the winds blow through the sky ;"

for the best and our favourite place from which to watch

> " When the great sunset burned itself away,"

was the top of this bank. The view here is truly magnificent, and has been well described by Macdonald in his rambles. Smith was still standing in imagination here, and painting from nature —recording what he had actually seen when he wrote—

> " From yonder trees I've seen the western sky
> All washed with fire, while, in the midst, the sun
> Beat like a pulse, welling at ev'ry beat
> A spreading wave of light."

The photograph of that particular sunset still hangs fresh in my mind, and I also retain a vivid recollection of that which immediately follows the above lines—

> " Where yonder church
> Stands up to heaven, as if to intercede
> For sinful hamlets scattered at its feet,
> I saw the dreariest sight," etc. (Life Drama, pp. 51, 52.)

In the second volume of " A Summer in Skye," Smith has described Kenmuir, and in narrating a ramble to it, records an incident that happened several years before he had first visited the Hebrides. It may not be out of place to repeat it here, seeing he has omitted in his report one of his own characteristic smart sayings on the occasion. We had walked together from the city along the river side as far as Dalbeth Burn, near Harvey's Dyke, when we beheld a plain but tidily dressed old, good-looking, matronly woman, and a sprightly boy about twelve years of age, standing in embarrassment, because of recent floods having carried away the plank which had bridged the still swollen streamlet. We assisted them over their difficulty, and having received may thanks, pushed on towards Carmyle and Kenmuir, leaving them behind. At length, having spent some time in the wood, we again reached the village on our return. " But what is to do ? The children are gathered in a circle, and the wives are standing at the open doors. There is a performance going on. The

tambourine is sounding, and a tiny acrobat, with a
fillet round his brow, tights covered with tinsel
lozenges, and flesh coloured shoes, is striding
about on a pair of stilts, to the no small amuse-
ment and delight of the juveniles. He turns his
head," and I had no sooner said—" 'Tis the boy of
Dalbeth Burn," than Smith, laying one hand on
my shoulder, and pointing with the other to the
sylph-like form poised in the air, whispered in
my ear, " Be not forgetful to entertain strangers ;
for some "—laying emphasis on the last word—
" have entertained angels unawares."* But we are
recognised : the boy smiles and honours us with a
graceful salute ;—the old lady, too, gives the
tambourine a few special beats, and drops us one
of her best curtsies, and, as we have become " the
observed of all observers," we make a hasty
retreat.

---

* Smith was often very happy at a *bon mot* of this kind. On
another occasion, for example, when we were passing through the
village of Camlachie, a group of women and boys were assembled
round a milk cart, the owner of which was engaged in an angry

But Smith was certainly not gifted with prophetic vision when he wrote in his second volume of "A Summer in Skye," regarding Carmyle—"an old, quiet, sleepy place, where nothing has happened for the last fifty years, and where nothing will happen for fifty years to come." And I suspect he had not visited the village for several years, or he would not have written further— "For half a century not one stone has been placed upon another here;" for, on revisiting Carmyle a

---

altercation with a ragged little urchin ; and having a large measure full of buttermilk in his hand, he dashed the whole contents in his rage on the boy's face—"Eh, that's a *sour douk*," said Smith.　And again, during one of the brief visits he paid to Glasgow, after he was located in Edinburgh, being accosted on the street by a member of the Addisonian Society with a—"Well, have you come back for a change of air?"　"No, I have only come for a change of smoke," was his quick reply.　At another time, a member of the same club, being engaged during one of its sittings, on the opposite side of a debate from him, finished a long argument rather inelegantly, by saying "that is the right stuff;" "and it is *stuff*," retorted Smith, without rising from his seat.　Such ejacu-
.lations of spontaneous wit were frequent with him in the club. Indeed, it was generally thus that he answered his opponents, for he never excelled in argumentation.

few months after his death, I found several new houses had been added to the village since he and I used to pass through it, while some old ones had undergone considerable alteration, in order to render them more conformable to modern taste. A railway, too, had been carried through the district, and a station built at only a short distance from this loveliest and loneliest village of the Clyde. It therefore requires no seer's gift to foretell that, long before the fifty years during which nothing is to happen here, the Carmyle of to-day shall have altogether passed away. The change has already begun; and I confess that, while I found a considerable advantage in being conveyed in a few minutes by rail to Carmyle on this occasion, it pained me to behold the station, and especially to witness the alterations made and making in the old-fashioned village. There was one house, however, on which happily time had wrought no change, and which I passed with very peculiar feelings. This was the very humble but always clean refreshment house, where Smith and

I were wont to partake of bread and cheese and porter, on our way home from Kenmuir. I felt strongly inclined to enter, and sit alone for a while in its large sombre room with white sanded floor, that I might meditate on the past, and try to realize in imagination

> "The touch of a vanished hand,
>   And the sound of a voice that is still."

But time and other considerations forbade the gratification of this melancholy longing on the present occasion; so I passed on through the village to the Clyde, and turned towards Kenmuir. It was nearly fifteen years since I had been here before along with Mr. Smith. Indeed, often as I had once frequented the place, I had seldom been there but in his company, and all my associations of it were consequently connected with him. Therefore, as I at length entered the wooded bank, and began to thread the winding footpath, there came upon my spirit one of the strangest and most powerful experiences of my life. All in this

once so familiar scene was so much the same as of
old. The trees had grown no greater ; there they
stood, at angles of the path, with their unchanged
features. No additional shrub, even, seemed to
be added to the tangle. The very blades of grass
seemed just the same blades. The old flowers
had not died—there they were in their wonted
spots. All was so startlingly familiar that I felt
as if I had renewed my youth ; the past was
restored ; the intervening years became a vanished
dream. At one moment I could not resist obey-
ing an impulse to turn round and make sure that
Smith was not behind me. Had I then seen his
form, I do not think it would have surprised
me much ; nor had I heard him pronounce my
name, would it have startled me. My imagination
was in that state of heat and tension in which
apparitions may be begotten. My progress
through the wood gave me a fuller understanding
than I had previously—a kind of realization,
indeed—of "the valley of the shadow of death."
I felt as if accompanied through "all the lonely

greenery of the place" by the spirit of my departed friend. Yet there was no fearfulness upon my heart. I was filled with solemn enjoyment. It was a powerful experience, which I had in no measure anticipated. It came upon me suddenly by the singularly-familiar look of all surrounding objects linking me anew to the past ; and I do not believe it could be repeated again to the same degree of intensity by another visit to the same scene. The feeling subsided, not as it came, but gradually, as I approached the end of the bank. I then sat down by the side of the well, and tried to recall the sweetly-solemn impression, by summoning my imagination to seat the loved form as of old on the opposite side of the well, but in vain. I then retraced the path for a short distance, and perceived that several trees had their barks sculptured with the initial letters of names far more thickly than they used to be. This was a clear indication that Smith's poems and Macdonald's book of "Rambles," had given a notoriety to the place which it did not formerly possess. And this surmise was speedily confirmed by entering into conversation with the tenant of the land, whom I found sitting under a tree at the top of the bank, as I left the wood. On remarking that it used to be a very lonely spot, for on often visiting it in years past I scarcely ever met any person in it; "Oh," said he, "it is not so now, for within the last few years it has many visitors, and especially on the Sabbaths, when it has far too many." On being further asked if he knew of any cause of this increase of visitors, he said "No," and appeared to be ignorant of Smith and Macdonald having celebrated his farm in their writings. I had observed, also, before leaving the wood, that its former, and natural silence, was ever and anon disturbed by the puff and whistle of railway engines, so that the following sentence by Smith —"The shallow wash and murmur of the Clyde flows through a silence as deep as that of an American wilderness," is already out of date. *Sic tempora mutantur !*

By starting from Queen Street at 4 o'clock p.m.,
our Saturday afternoon's excursions were occasionally extended farther than Kenmuir. One place
in particular, thus visited once or twice each
summer, was Bothwell Priory. In going thither
we sometimes walked by the northern bank of
the Clyde, as far as the bridge which spans the
river a mile or so below that hoary ruin, and then
pursued the rest of the way along the south bank.
This necessitated our fording the Calder, which
we did by one wading and carrying the other
on his back. But as this route involved other
disadvantages, among which were the ordinary
risks of trespassers, we more frequently, with regret
at being separated from the much-loved Clyde,
went by the London road, and returned by
Cambuslung and Rutherglen. An occasional
summer holiday was sometimes also spent at the
Priory in reading the poets; and I have a very
specially endeared remembrance of us passing
one such day in autumn, while the reapers were
busy in the golden grain, in Campsie's most

romantic glen.   There we lay for hours, under the cloudless sky, upon a jutting bossy rock below one of the falls, during which time Smith read the whole of Thomson's "Castle of Indolence," and never was poem read in more auspicious scene and circumstance, or more appreciated.

CHAPTER IV.

The Highlands.

"This rambling strain
Recalls our summer walks again ;
When doing nought—and to speak true,
Not anxious to find aught to do,—
The wild unbounded hills we ranged,
While oft our talk its topic changed ;
And desultory as our way,
Ranged, unconfined, from grave to gay."

SCOTT.

AS Smith was allowed a week of holidays each summer, we began in 1848 spending it together in excursions to the Highlands. Our first trip was to the island of Arran. We set out on a Monday morning in July.

"The morn rose blue and glorious o'er the world ;
The steamer left the black and oozy wharves,
And floated down between dark ranks of masts.

And at length in Brodick Bay,

> " We reached the pier,
> Whence girls in fluttering dresses, shady hats,
> Smiled rosy welcome "—

not to us, however. We were strangers to all. Our means did not permit us putting up at the fashionable hotel. But this was no hardship; for the gay company and bustle of the place would not have been at all congenial to our young and rather solitary spirits; so we sought for a private lodging, and with considerable difficulty—for the little town was overcrowded with tourists and summer visitors—found a house where one bedroom might be had; and as this entirely suited both our purse and our inclination, we took it for a week. On the following morning we walked along the shore to Glen Sannox, where we spent the whole long summer day, by turns walking, climbing, and lying on the heather; conversing much on many topics, and particularly on the superstitions of the Highlanders and

F

islanders of Scotland, as Smith has indicated in
the following lines :—

> "The beauty of the morning drew me on
> Into a gloomy glen.   The heavy mists
> Crept up the mountain-sides.   I heard the streams ;
> The place was saddened with the bleat of sheep.
> 'Tis surely in such lonely scenes as these
> Mythologies are bred.   The rolling storms—
> The mountains standing black in mist and rain,
> With long white lines of torrents down their sides—
> The ominous thunder creeping up the sky—
> The homeless voices at the dead of night
> Wandering among the glens—the ghost-like clouds
> Stealing beneath the moon,—are but as stuff
> Whence the awe-stricken herdsman could create
> Gods for his worship."

Other glens were also visited, and the hills were
climbed, but we were prevented reaching the
top of Goatfell by the gathering of a thunder
storm.   On the whole, however, the weather
was fine during our holidays, and we had a
season of intense enjoyment.   It was the first
trip we had taken together, and so highly were
we delighted with it, that it was resolved, as we
lay one day in Glen Sannox, that, if spared till

next summer, we would take a pedestrian tour together through some part of the Highlands— Smith insisting, as a special part of the agreement, that no third person should be of the party. By this time we had come to understand each other, and both of us found our rambles most agreeable and profitable when no other friend was present. Indeed, it was a peculiar characteristic of Smith that, while he could be social and enjoy select society, he found far most delight himself, and his conversation was most rich and captivating when with only one genial friend. To know him, you required to have him for a while by himself. And if you were happy enough to secure this occasionally, you could not but love him for the rest of your life in a more than ordinary degree. This characteristic he retained until his death.

In accordance with the above agreement, in July of the following year (1849),

> "Like clouds or streams we wandered on at will
> Three glorious days."

Travelling first by train to Stirling—accompanied .by a friend and his betrothed—we spent several hours visiting the Castlehill and the other places of historic and natural interest about the town, and paid a hasty visit to the field of Bannockburn ; then, knapsack on back, and stick in hand, we turned our faces towards Benledi, under whose shade we had resolved to sleep that night, and began our journey on foot to Callander. Our friends accompanied us as far as Bridge of Allan—at that time a small and humble village, lovely indeed, but very unlike the present gay resort of invalids. At length we reached Doune, where "A Duke of Albany lost his head in view of the Castle : a blind trout lives in its well, and visitors feel more interested in the trout than in the duke." So we, like other visitors, bent down over the well, and being favoured with the sight of "a shadow on the sandy bottom, and the twinkle of a fin," pursued our journey, and finally reached Callander, as Smith has related thus,—" It was sunset

as I approached it first—years ago. Beautiful
the long crooked street of white-washed houses,
dressed in rosy colours. Prettily dressed children were walking or running about. 'The empty
coach was standing at the door of the hotel,
and the smoking horses were being led up
and down. And right in front stood King
Benledi clothed in imperial purple, the spokes
of splendour from the sinking sun raying far
into heaven from behind his mighty shoulders."
Here we spent the following day—Sunday. In
the forenoon we attended Divine service in the
Free Church, where a peculiar incident occurred.
Before leaving our hotel, Smith engaged to put a
New Testament in his pocket to serve us both in
church. And having his attention fixed on some
object, thought, or person, as the minister at
length announced the first psalm, he put his hand
in his pocket and handed me the book, to look
up the place. But on opening the small volume,
instead of a New Testament with the psalms of
David, in metre, appended, I found it to be a copy

of "Don Juan," and immediately handed it back
to him open at the title-page.   Having glanced
at it and seen his mistake, our eyes met, and the
grotesque idea of the "Don" in church, destroyed
for a space, I fear, becoming solemnity in both
our minds.

In the afternoon we walked up the pass of
Leney to Loch Lubnaig, feeling on our spirits the
spell of Scott's muse; for we were now in the
scene of "The Lady of the Lake."

"Benledi saw the cross of fire"

carried through this pass by young Angus of
Duncraggan, and delivered into the hands of
young Norman of Armandave, as the latter came
forth from the chapel of St. Bride leading the
fair Mary of Tombea from the altar, where she
had pledged to him her troth.

But even Scott was destined to be soon forgot,
while thoughts and feelings more in harmony with
the sacred day were awakened within us, as before
we reached Lubnaig, "the lake of the rueful

countenance," we came suddenly upon a place unnoticed in guide-books, which made a deep impression upon our spirits—the most sombre and solitary of burial grounds—a true " God's acre " among the mountains, with no abode of living man in sight. Smith has several times alluded to this spot in his works. In the second volume of " A Summer in Skye," he writes of it thus,—" Beside the road is an old churchyard, for which no one seems to care—the tombstones being submerged in a sea of rank grass." In " A Life Drama," he describes it as—

" The still, old graveyard 'mong the dreary hills ;"

and in " A Boy's Poem," as—

" A churchyard covered with forgetful grass."

But the passage in which he has specially referred to it occurs in that exquisite little poem, which he incorporated in " A Life Drama," but as originally composed, was entitled "The Garden and the Child," and regarding which the Rev.

George Gilfillan wrote, on reading it in MS.,—
"Which *must* be published. It reminds us of the
style of Wordsworth's finer ballads, and has made
us both weep and thrill." In his "Gallery of
Literary Portraits," too, he has said of it,—"Which
alike we and the author consider the best strain
in the whole 'Life Drama.' It was the perusal of
it which first increased to certainty our previous
notion that Mr. Smith was one of our truest poets."
The following lines contain the record of our
visit to this "still, old graveyard":—

> "By the shores of Loch Lubnaig,
>   A dear friend and I were walking
>   ('Twas the Sabbath,) we were talking
>   Of dreams and feelings vague ;
>   We paused by a place of graves,
>   Scarcely a word was 'twixt us given,
>   Silent the earth, silent the heaven,
>   No murmur of the waves,
>   The awed loch lay black and still
>   In the black shadow of the hill.
>   We loosed the gate and entered in," etc.

This, in truth, we did both on going and returning, and spent some time among the graves. But,

of course, the eclipse of the sun, described as witnessed there, was not seen *corporis oculis*, but only by the poet's "vision and faculty divine."

I retain in my possession a letter from Smith of this year, which contains this charming lyric as originally written. The letter begins thus—

Friday Night.

MY DEAR T——,

I hereby send you a poem, a phantom of heart and brain, composed very rapidly, in a most diabolical mood, when I might have said, regarding my inner man,

" Hell is empty,
And all the devils are here."

. . . It is not very long. The rhymes may be bad, but . . . it was writ in two hours.

A. SMITH.

This is interesting, as showing the rapidity with which he could write such verses at the early age of nineteen. But the poem was thus quickly composed, because it was written under a true and powerful inspiration, which came upon him under the following circumstances :—It happened, on the day of its composition, that he was, as described in the above letter, in one of those melancholy moods to which he was often subject in those days, without any very definite cause, and, in returning from dinner along the Trongate to his work, he came upon a bright, rosy, laughing little girl, " beautiful as heaven," and the sight of her sweet, happy innocence thrilled his heart, fired his imagination, and awoke all the music of his soul. All the afternoon he was silent at his desk. The child was still before him ; his imagination brooded over her beauty in musing reverie, and more and more his soul glowed before the breath of inspiration, till eight o'clock, when he went straight and in silence from the warehouse to his room in Charlotte Street, and, lifting his pen, allowed his heated, pent up thoughts to rush into the mould of poetry. In comparing my copy as thus written that night with the piece as it now occurs in " A Life Drama," I find a number of verbal emendations, most of which, though, as I think, not all, are improvements. In one place, also, three verses have been expunged, and others inserted in their stead, while three new verses have been added. But—I know not well how to account for it,—I am never so affected when I read this piece as part of "A Life Drama," as when I read it in accordance with its original composition, as an isolated lyric. It seems to have suffered, as I regard several of the author's other early poems did, even to a greater extent, by unnatural incorporation in, and unfavourable juxtaposition with, other portions of the "Life Drama." When I read this piece as published, I confess that Mr. Gilfillan's eulogium of it seems excessive, but it never does so when I read it *as he did*, when he commended it—as an isolated and independent poem. Every time I peruse my copy in the letter before me, I am affected with deep and varied emotions; and often very much regret that Mr. Smith was not content to appear, at the beginning, before the world simply as a lyrist. Had he done so, I believe he would to-day have occupied a unique and unrivalled position in the kingdom of poets.

But to return to our narrative. After a hasty visit to the Bridge of Bracklin, we were, on the following morning, on our way to the Trossachs by an early hour,—for we had a long day's journey in prospect.

The morning was of doubtful promise. Huge masses of clouds hurried after each other across the sky, and we were consequently apprehensive of rain. Under this feeling we had not proceeded far till we came upon an aged Highlander working upon the road, from whom we were favoured with the only attempt I have heard a Highland peasant, in his native wilds, make at wit. After addressing him with the usual good morning, one of us asked,—"Do you think we shall have rain?" "I ha'e nae doubt o't," was his reply, which having caused us—with our townsmen's ideas of a mountaineer's powers of prognosticating by the signs of the sky—to hesitate whether we should retrace our steps or hasten our speed onwards, we ventured the further inquiry—"Do you think it will be soon?" when he responded, "Ah, I canna jist say, but I'm sure it 'll rain sometime; an' a bad business it would be if it did na." Whether the Scottish Highlanders are endowed with wit or not I know not; but if they are, they do not exercise the faculty much before strangers. Wit is generally allied with sprightliness and volubility, but the Highlander at home is taciturn and morose. But amused rather at Donald's effort than his success, we pushed on, and soon under the double spell of Scott and nature—romance and reality,

> " We walked 'mid unaccustomed sights and sounds;
>   Fair apparitions of the elements
>   That lived a moment on the air, then passed
>   To the eternal world of memory :"

for the spirit of the prince of novelists seemed to haunt the scene opening every moment in fuller beauty before us. The rolling clouds casting alternate shade and sunshine on the gorgeous landscape, only varied and enhanced its effects upon our minds. It would be impossible to describe our emotions. They were varied; sometimes awing, but more generally jubilant. At one moment, in what is properly the Trossach's pass, our spirits sought vent in shouting lustily, and so woke to our surprise the reverberating echoes of the hills; and as peak after peak thus unexpectedly answered to our voices, our hearts were filled with a new joy. Never before nor after did I see Smith so excited. It is not to be wondered, therefore, that he has marked the spot, in his works, thus—"Echo sits babbling beneath the rock;" and also recorded the fact as follows, in a "A Boy's Poem,"—

> We raised a shout,
> A sullen echo—then were heard the sweet
> And skiey tones of spirits 'mid the peaks,
> Faint voice to faint voice shouting; dim halloos
> From unseen cliff and ledge; and answers came
> From some remoter region far withdrawn
> Within the pale blue sky."

But at length, in all its loveliness, Loch Katrine

burst upon our view, and we sat down by its brink and gazed a while on Helen's Isle. No boat nor form of any kind was visible upon its waters, and no voice, no sound was heard. The July sun shining unclouded now in its full strength, caused even the birds of song to seek the covert of the woods, and hushed the voice of nature, while it spread a splendour over all the scene. To rest and lie in reverie indeed were sweet, but could not be long indulged. Having heroically resolved to be true pedestrians, we determined to have nothing to do with the steamer on Loch Katrine, but to walk the whole length of the classic lake—round its head, and rest for the night at Tarbet on Loch Lomond. And this purpose we accomplished. Towards the end of our journey, however, the clouds which had been gathering for some time began to distil a soaking rain, as the following extract from a sonnet relates :—

Near our journey's end,
As down the moorland road we straight did wend,

　　　To Wordsworth's Inversneyd, talking to kill
　　　The cold and cheerless drizzle in the air,
　　　'Bove me I saw—at pointing of my friend—
　　　An old fort, like a ghost upon the hill,
　　　Stare in blank misery through the blinding rain ;
　　　So human-like it seemed in its despair—
　　　So stunned with grief—long gazed at it we twain."

From Inversneyd we were rowed over to Tarbet by two greedy Highlanders, who did not fail, from our inexperience, to fleece us a little. At Tarbet we lodged for the night, and next day proceeded to Inverary, by Arrochar, round the head of Loch Long and through Glen Croe, in which we experienced the drenching powers of a Scotch mist. Seated at length on the celebrated "rest and be thankful" under the heavy dusk and soaking atmosphere, a woman, blind of one eye and bare of foot, with a miserable-looking child tied on her back by an old tartan plaid, came suddenly upon us through the mist, and on being asked if it always rained up here, replied, "No, it's shist this way." The mist at length rolled away as we hied onward, and, under a good breeze, our

clothes dried on us before we reached Loch
Fyne ; and having been ferried across to Inverary,
we took steamer the following morning to Glasgow, where we arrived in due time, with scarcely
a shilling between us ; but, in truth, we had not
one pound sterling each when we started.

CHAPTER V.

𝕽𝖊𝖛𝖊𝖑𝖆𝖙𝖎𝖔𝖓𝖘.

" A prophecy and intimation,
    A pale and feeble adumbration."

LONGFELLOW.

I HAD by this time become aware of Smith's devotion to poetry. Indeed, there were few secrets between us now. A friendship more close and sincere could scarcely exist between two persons. He was silent, however, for a considerable time after I became acquainted with him, regarding his writing poetry. At first he repeated a few lines occasionally in our evening rambles. At length it became a practice, when three or more of the select of the Addisonian club met together for a stroll by Clyde side, for each to repeat from memory the finest passages of the poets, on some particular subject,

that he recollected. And, on these occasions,
Smith sometimes quietly introduced a few lines
of his own, in order to see how they were appreciated—concealing, of course, the authorship.
And as I had generally heard them before, I preserved a friendly reticence. On being requested
to name the author, an evasive answer was given.
Sometimes, too, he indulged in a little mischiev-
ous humour by extemporising a stanza of no
great merit, in order to try his critics. One night,
for example, each was repeating passages on Love,
and Smith, after having quoted numerous fine
passages, pretending to have forgotten the authorship, repeated the following lines, which were ex-
temporised by himself :—

> " 'Tis sad to sleep 'neath the cold black loam,
>   'Tis sad from this world to part ;
> But sadder far 'tis to have no home,
>   No home in a human heart."

And he was much amused by the most sober
minded of the company expressing unbounded
admiration, and demanding their repetition that

they might be imprinted indelibly on his memory. And, indeed, the praise then bestowed thus upon them seems for a while to have caused Smith to regard them favourably himself; for I find them in his own handwriting in a serious poem I have by me, which was cut down, and in great part used up again piecemeal, in the compilation of "A Life Drama."

I had no idea, however, of how much he had written till the following incident occurred :—Not finding him as usual at our meeting-place one evening, and learning from one of his fellow-workers that he had not been in the warehouse that day, I suspected that he might be unwell, as he had complained the previous night of a slight cold ; and on the following morning I had a note from him stating that such was the case, and re-questing me as he had no intention of leaving home that day either, to visit him in the evening. I consequently did call upon him in the evening, when I found him seated alone in his snug little room before the fire. We had a long talk together. He seemed all the while, however, in an abstracted mood. I suspected there was something on his mind which he desired to communicate, and endeavoured in various ways to lead him into freer conversation. But all being in vain, I at length rose to leave, when he suddenly also rose to his feet, saying, "Sit down a little : I have something that I wish to show you." He then went to a drawer and took out a mass of manuscript, and, sitting down again, began to read from it with a rather tremulous voice. I was soon captivated and astonished. When he was done reading, we sat for some moments in silence ; for I was as one bewildered with surprise. Had I spoken as I then felt, I should have expressed myself, perhaps too warmly, only in unmeasured terms of laudation, and so have chanced to offend him ; for he utterly disliked flattery. At length, having abruptly said, "I had no idea that you had written so much," he replied, "Well, but what do you think of it?" "Think of it," I answered, "I know not what to think or say of

it just now; but this I will say," rising from emotion and taking his hand, "go on and do take
care of these manuscripts; for I believe the
world will love to read them, and may ask for
them soon." And so I turned to leave, while he,
pressing my hand with much feeling, said, "I
understand and thank you. Let us say no more
at present. We shall be able to speak more freely
of this again." So we parted. But next night we
met again, and finding that we could speak more
freely then, had a long and interesting conversation on life's purposes and aims, in connection
with, and as suggested by, the preceding night's
revelation. But still feeling that I could better
express my thoughts to him by writing than
viva voce, I addressed to him—as we were both
wont to do on special occasions—a letter, of
which I kept no copy, and the contents of which
I cannot now recall. The following answer,
however, will reveal so far its nature, and,
what is of more importance, also account for a
fact in his life to which reference has already

been made, both in these pages and by other writers.

"Monday Evening.

"DEAR TOM,

"As we talked this night last week, few stars were visible in my spirit sky; those visible looked dreary and cold. One has gone out since. Let it go. A star, 'my life's star,' burneth, and *will* burn : when it sets, I set.

"Your letter, I need not say, was read with interest. You have my sincere thanks. You have been very frank with me of late; I will return you like for like. I will unclasp my soul to you, and you may read what I had hoped one day to have avowed proudly; or, that hope failing, to have buried it for ever—a dead hope in a dead heart.

"You may recollect, on the evening which has given rise to this epistle, you made a guess as to what mine aspirations tended—you guessed poetry. I made some evasive answer. I could not then say 'Ay.' I can *now* say you guessed aright.

It has been the seventh heaven of my aspirations for years; a passion running as deep as the aboriginal waters of my being.   At the present moment the 'passion poesy' standeth on the necks óf all the others like a king, and it will ultimately swallow them as the serpent of Moses swallowed the serpents of the Egyptian magicians.   It is with a feeling of humiliation I make this confession.   I know not how *you* will receive it, I trust, however, you will do me justice in your thoughts; that you will not place me in the category with the D——s, K——s, J——s.   I believe my spirit is something different from theirs —deeper and sincerer.   I am unconscious of that pitiful vanity (the Alpha and Omega of their hopes) to see one's name in print ; the immortality of five minutes in the 'poet's corner.'   Above all, don't laugh or sneer, however much you may pity. I could bear sneers on this point from no one, least of all from you.   I might keep silent, but I would suffer like a martyr in his shirt of fire. Believe me it's no laughing matter.   Underneath those wide doming heavens, that ancient sun, those pitying stars, of all the miseries this is the chiefest —when one has the soul, blood, heart, pulses of an angel—all but the wings! This is egotism with a vengeance, but we are all egotists; and all we are, feel or see—this universe of souls, stars and suns, is but a sublime egotism of Deity.

"You tell me you wish I should yet fill a pulpit: this may never be. I speak in sober sadness when I say I am unfit for public life. That fire once burnt brightly on the hearthstone of my heart—the flame flickered, waned, and died; a mighty wind scattered the red embers like autumn leaves: the hearthstone is now cold; I do not wish to fill a pulpit.

"You may be inclined to ask, 'What do you intend to do?' I might say, 'Nothing.' To attempt to become a preacher is useless: incapacity *within—without* difficulties no capacity could overcome—prevent it. What I would like is just some way of living which would feed and cover this carcase, and allow much time to roam through book-world, and the world of my own spirit, like the new-born Adam in the new-born Eden. You may say this life I desire to lead will not be a useful one for my fellows. Granted ! I do not intend to gird on an apron and become waiter to the world.

"If you judge me by the length of my letter you may think me rather ungrateful. I am at the confessional, and, *certes*, the confession is no pleasant task. I do not know, however, that anything more need be said. I have unbosomed myself as well as I could. I fear this night's work will lessen your esteem for me, as I have fallen somewhat in my own in the course of it. If it so be, I will be the only loser. Jog along, Tom ; the road of life is rough, but the eternities are ahead. We will reach them soon.

"Yours truly,

A. Smith."

The sentiment with which this letter concludes —" the eternities are ahead : we shall reach them soon," was from Smith's pen, no merely flippant saying. As several persons have already noticed, he has in his writings, with singular plainness and frequency, expressed forebodings of a premature death. The couplet,—

> " Before me runs a road of toil
> With my grave cut across,"

has since his death been repeatedly quoted in instance of this. But his works do not express this feeling more frequently than his conversation did from the first day that I knew him. The general tenor of his youth was by no means melancholy; still, in our private walks and conferences he was ever and anon uttering this gloomy presentiment. But the following poetical epistle which he sent me this winter, when our regular meetings were again restricted to the Saturday afternoon, exhibits it so fully as seems to warrant its being published.*

---

* In publishing it, however, it is desirable that the reader understand, that though in my judgment it is a production not unworthy

The poet was, in this instance, alas! a true *vates*—a prophet. The epistle is headed—

"A DREAM.

"I had a dream, wrapt in prophetic sleep
The picture of a lifetime passed before me.
I saw a youth,
And he was not a stranger; for he seemed
To bear resemblance to myself or you.
His heart was bared before me, and I saw
The deepest secrets of his inmost soul,
His thoughts, his feelings, his emotions—all.
I started, for methought they were my own,
And so I loved him—'twas a fearful love.
He sought not much companionship,
And his close intimates had never dreamed
He was so strange a being. None could guess,
From what he said or did, the wild idolatry
Which reigned within. He worshipped intellect
Most fervently, and his young heart longed
High to be marshalled 'mongst the mighty dead.

of Smith's early muse, it is not given here as a specimen of his poetic talent. It would be altogether improper to print it as such, seeing it was evidently written off rapidly at óne sitting, and was never designed by him for the press. It would néver, therefore, have been put in type by me had it not, apart entirely from its not inconsiderable poetic value, been specially interesting as a prophecy now singularly and sadly fulfilled.

He was a lonely being, a dreamer strange,
He mingled with the whirl of human life—
A mingler masked.   He was not what he seemed ;
(But, ah ! *he was unmasked*, and his pale brow
Dewy with death-sweat gleams upon me now)
He had no sympathy with the rude world :
His world was in himself ; and with his dreams—
Most gorgeous dreams—he sported years away.
          He loved not company,
Nor was he solitary, for nature spake
Most musically to his listening ear—
The lull of waters and the sighing breeze.
At eventide—the holy twilight stealing on,
The flowers, the waving grass, the sunset sky,
Streaked with rich purple—all these had a voice.
And when the glorious night o'erspread the world
With her dark wings, distilling pearly dew
Upon the thirsty flowers, how passing sweet
Were then his wanderings no man can tell ;
For star-born melody came floating by ;
His tranced ear drank music spiritually wild.
Night was holy—the full-orbed moon
Rolled on her bright path through the deep blue sky,
Bathing the landscape in her silvery light ;
And one thin fleecy cloud which onward sailed,
Tinged by her rays, seemed like a spirit's home.
And the wild gleaming stars which lit the vault
Of heaven—the myriad toned voice of night,
Roused up a tide of passion in his soul
Which may be felt—which words can never tell.

When stirred by more than mortal sympathies,
When his own heart-strings thrilled to nature's melody,
When poetry rolled o'er him like a flood,
Had he met then an every-day companion,
All, all was stilled, and for a time he seemed
To be a soulless mass like those around him.

  * * * * * *

This vision vanished, and another came.
Years had rolled on, and he was now a man.
His dark hair clustered on his death-like brow,
Startlingly pale, and his deep sunk eye,
Alas ! 'twas sadly changed since days of yore !
Seldom he smiled ! but oh ! that ghastly smile
Illumed the brow of agony !　Where now
Were all his pantings after future fame—
His dreams of boyhood—were they realized ?
Yes he won a name, but—lost himself,
For death's barbed arrow quivered in his heart.
Soon he would be numbered with the mighty dead ;
Soon he would be voiceless—yet the echo
Of his voice would speak for evermore.
     His fame now seemed
To his fast flitting soul an empty dream ;
Undying laurels on a fleshless brow ;
A golden halo o'er a grinning skull.
I sadly gazed upon that half-known face,
And felt as if my doom were shadowed there.

  * * * * * *

   'Tis the stilly hush of midnight,
The sighing wind is mute, and not a sound

Floats on the air.   How glorious this scene !
All things imbued with the moon's cold beam,
Silvery and pure !   The starry-fretted vault
Of midnight heaven, with its rich pageantry,
Is scarce more lovely than the sleeping earth.
The nodding woods flash back the moonbeams pale,
And these quiet, moveless waters, at this hour
Appear like sheeted silver.
         I stood beside a grave :
It was *his* grave ; and there I stood, as if
Some fearful secret was to be revealed.
His tomb was far remote from cities' hum ;—
He never loved their bustle, and his grave
Was midst that nature which he loved so well.
The grass was spangled with the glittering dew,
And the sweet-scented violets had a tear
Gleaming upon their face.   The modest daisy,
And all the flowers which bloomed around his grave,
Were clad in grief—all wet with nature's tears.
I thought upon the mouldering dead, and wept.
His life was brief, yet glorious ; and now
All that remained was lying 'neath my feet.
I looked upon the gravestone, and on it
Was carved—'Here lies an Addisonian.'
My life-blood curdled, and my trembling limbs
Could not support me.   I fell—and woke,
The chilly sweat standing on my fevered brow.
O God, is this the shadow of my destiny ! "

                  A. Smith.

But not one line of Mr. Smith's had as yet appeared in print. He was in no such haste as juvenile poets generally are to rush into type. He had for several years written such poetry as few could write, before any, except his nearest relatives and one or two of his most intimate and confidential friends, knew that he had composed one stanza. This was, perhaps, the result unitedly of ambition and diffidence. He was ambitious of his productions having more than an ephemeral existence in some newspaper or magazine, and at the same time sensitively afraid of their being either rejected or regarded as merely mediocre. So

> " Studious of song
> And yet ambitious not to sing in vain,"

he wrote on, re-wrote often, and long reserved.

CHAPTER VI.

The Highlands, Love, and Aspirations.

> " We marked each memorable scene,
>   And held poetic talk between ;
>   Nor hill nor brook we paced along
>   But had its legend or its song."
>
> *   *   *   *   *
>
>   " Since oft thy praise
>   Hath given fresh vigour to my lays ;
>   Since oft thy judgment could refine
>   My flattened thought, or cumbrous line,
>   Still kind, as is thy wont, attend."
>
> SCOTT.

IN the month of July of next year, after spending a day or two as guests of a mutual friend
at Strone, we started on the second of our
pedestrian tours through the Highlands. Our
brief sojourn at Strone was a pleasant and
profitable one. Holy Loch became much endeared to us by its surpassing loveliness, and,
consequently, was several times visited in after

H

years. Comparing it with the other Scottish lochs, Smith says, "Smallest and loveliest of them all." It is a famous haunt of landscape painters, and on this occasion we met on its shore John Cairns, a painter of no little merit, between whose death and that of Smith only a few months elapsed. I had the pleasure of introducing them at this time to each other. On the afternoon of our arrival at Strone, we took a walk together to the village of Kilmun, and on returning rested for some time on the green sward, under the shade of some noble trees near the coast road. Each seemed to be a great bee-hive. The murmuring hum of the insects, blending with the murmuring surge of the adjacent waters, was to us a new and exquisite sensation, and we lay long enjoying it. The impression was not lost on Smith. His readers may remember the following allusion among others :—

> "I lay beneath a glimmering sycamore,
>   Drowsy with murmuring bees."

It was also while lying, on the following day, on

the beach, a little farther down the loch, and
watching the flow and reflux of the tidal waves,
that the following original, much and justly
admired figure was begotten in the poet's mind.
After a few moments of silent, thoughtful gazing,
he quietly stretched out his hand, a sweet smile
lighting up his countenance, and said, almost in
these very words,—

> " See, the bridegroom sea,
> Is toying with the shore, his wedded bride ;
> And in the fulness of his marriage joy,
> He decorates her tawny brow with shells ;—
> Retires a space, to see how fair she looks,
> Then proud runs up to kiss her."

This became a favourite image with him. It is
repeated in various forms, less fully drawn out,
four times at least in " A Life Drama " alone. It
was thus spontaneously, while looking upon some
object, that almost all his finest metaphors were
acquired, and not during study at his desk. They
came, they were not excogitated. All nature was
to his mind full of symbols, and he was ever wake-
ful to discern and understand them. It was his

"chief joy to draw images from everything." As we could both on occasions walk together for miles without speaking, his mind at such times was always busy; and when any happy image presented itself to his imagination, he very generally, if no third person was present, gave immediate utterance to it. So frequently did this occur, that it constituted one of the richest charms of his society, and proved him to be truly a born poet, illustrating the lines,—

> " Familiar things enough to you and me
> Take a strange glory from the poet's mind."

When such ideas dawned upon the horizon of his mind, there were no manifestations of ecstacy or rapture made by him. There might, indeed, be seen a momentary sparkle in his eye, or glow upon his countenance, but there was no "fine frenzy rolling," and no airs,—all was quiet and natural. Nor did I ever see him on such occasions use any note-book. His memory was so tenacious that he fixed there his most transitory thoughts "in a sure place," to work out and polish at his leisure ; and I never heard him regret that he had forgotten any idea that had once been present to his mind. He regarded it, as one of the first laws of friendship, that any spontaneous thought which he thus expressed should not be repeated to others. The violation of this law gave him great offence, and he who rendered himself once guilty was not likely to be favoured with another opportunity of so transgressing.

From Strone we sailed across to Greenock, and went thence by steamer through the Kyles of Bute and Crinnan canal to Oban. On the following day we visited Dunstaffnage, Connal ferry, the vitrified fort of Berigonium ; and the next day sailed to Ballahulish at the mouth of Glencoe.

The coach for Loch Lomond stood in readiness for the passengers when we landed, but strapping our knapsack on our shoulders we started for the Glen on foot, before the coach, with the purpose of reaching Tyndrum that night. To see Glencoe was our chief object in this trip. Our expectations were great; but they were more than realized. We drank of the grandeur of the scenery till we were intoxicated with joy. Our minds became oppressed. The heat of the day, too, was intense. I shall never forget my emotions when the moor of Rannoch at length, "with its grey boulders," opened upon our view. We stood still, and "long gazed at it we twain." In due time we arrived at King's House, with keen appetites for dinner. And here we enjoyed an hour's rest. Then staff again in hand we resumed our journey. But after we had walked about two miles, Smith threw himself down on the grass by the road side, and stretched at full length we lay rather longer than I thought we could afford to do, seeing no house for a night's accommodation was to be expected nearer than the inn at Tyndrum. Ominous clouds, too, were gathering onwards, and several distant peals of thunder had been urging us to haste. So I endeavoured to stimulate my friend to arise, but to my surprise, for I had never seen him fail in walking before, he said he was too wearied, and was resolved to lie still where he was, and for once have a good sleep on the turf. This, however, I regarded as too hazardous to think of, and at length overcame his obstinacy by promising to endeavour to secure a bed, at least, for the night, in the first house we might come to, and so give up the idea of reaching Tyndrum till next day. We had to walk a few miles, however, before we found any house where we could have the accommodation required. And even then we had to put up, as a great favour, in a very humble and smoky highland hut. Here, however, we got a thoroughly clean bed in a very small room, and slept soundly till four o'clock next morning. At that hour I happened to awaken, and opening my eyes was startled at beholding a volume of blue smoke curling down through the top of the bed. My first impression was one of alarm. But having satisfied myself that the smoke was only coming, as a matter of course, from the peat fire which was already being kindled mid-floor the adjoining kitchen, and having opened the door of our room to allow it to escape, I awoke my friend, and pointing upwards to the smoke, he speedily stood upon the floor, under the impression that the house was on fire. Having dressed, and received some warm milk and oatmeal cakes from our kindly old hostess, who was already sitting enveloped in peat reek, with a black cutty pipe in her mouth, we started for Loch Lomond.   And, finally, from Tarbet took the steamer to Balloch, and proceeding thence by train to Bowling, and steamer to Glasgow, completed our tour for the year.   There is at least one allusion to the scene of this excursion in the drinking song sung by Arthur in " A Life Drama."

> " I've drank in Red Rannoch amidst its grey boulders,
>   Where fain to be kisst
>   Through his thin scarf of mist,
> Ben More to the sun heaves his wet shining shoulders."

It was in listening to the most noted elocutionist among the Addisonians reciting Motherwell's sword chant, that Smith conceived the purpose of writing that song in similar measure; and after composing it, having requested his oratorical friend to favour

him by reciting it, the whole club, and a few
friends, had the pleasure of hearing it recited at
the following annual *soiree* of the society.

The annual *soiree* of the Addisonian was quite
an event to us all in those days. It was an esta-
blished law of the club that no one should be ad-
mitted to that festival unless accompanied by a
lady; and as Smith and I were very seldom in
society, and consequently failed to cultivate acquaintance with the fair sex, this law gave us every
year a little annoyance. The other members came
to be aware of our embarrassment connected with
securing partners, and made it the subject of no
little mirthful banter. But Smith was sometimes,
I fear, involved in an unpleasant dilemma from
compliance with this rule; as, being wisely resolved
to remain free of any permanent attachment in his
present circumstances, but at the same time very
susceptible to female charms, he found it more
difficult to disengage himself from, than to procure
a partner. About this time, however, such a disen-
gagement was effected in a very melancholy man-

ner.   He had for some time been continuing to pay
attention to a young lady who had been with him
at our last annual gathering, and if I mistake not,
had agreed to meet her on a particular evening.
A dense fog, however, hung over the city all that
day, and when evening came the young lady failed
to be at the place of meeting : the thick darkness
and stifling condition of the atmosphere seemed to
him a sufficient reason for this.   But early on the
following day the mournful intelligence was brought
to him that she had been found that morning lying
dead in the Glasgow and Paisley canal.   On the
afternoon of the previous day, having made a call
at the southern extremity of the city, she had endeavoured to reach home the nearest way by going,
as she was accustomed to do often, for a short distance by the canal bank—although her friends had
advised her not to do so on this occasion ; and in
groping her way by the oft frequented path, she
must have fallen into the water.

But Smith has related the incident in the following passage of "A Boy's Poem" :—

" The fatal sun
Sucked vapours from the marsh. From morn till eve
The streets were huddled in a yellow fog,
Through which the lamps burned beamlessly and dim.

*   *   *   *   *

She sought relief in friends, and rose at last
With fond and hurried heart. They went with her.
' Don't take the river, cousin, 'tis so dark.'
' It is the shortest way—good night, good night.
They plead,—she broke from them—they called to her,—
She tossed a laughing answer from the dark.
The girls returned through thick-mist blinded streets,
And sat 'mid music in delighted rooms,
While she groped, weeping in night's foggy heart.

*   *   *   *   *

Hour passed on hour,
And gradually each apprehensive lip
Grew silent with concern ; then as they sat,
Like fern leaves troubled by a sudden wind,
Their hearts were stricken by a speechless fear ;—
Each read the terror in the other's face.
They searched with lights—they madly called her name ;—
Night heard, and, conscience-stricken, held its breath,
And listened wild. At length, in the bleared morn,
They saw a something white within the stream,—
He raised his drowned bride in distracted arms."

This unfortunate young lady possessed a singularly gentle disposition, combined with thoughtfulness of mind. Smith was only acquainted with

her for a brief period, and after her melancholy
death he evidently disliked to hear her spoken of,
and I never endeavoured to ascertain what impression she had made upon his heart.   He did not
seem, however, to have entertained any tenderer
affection than that of friendship, though he certainly esteemed her very highly, and his sorrow
at her lamentable death was sincere and poignant.
For several days he shunned all society.   On the
night of the day on which he had seen her remains
interred, we walked together for several miles
beyond the city, but he was indisposed for conversation, and I allowed him to indulge his sad
and solemn thoughts in silence.   He was of a
very sensitive and sympathetic nature, and on
this occasion it was more deeply moved to sadness
than I had seen it previously.

As a short time after this sad event we
walked together by Clydeside, he repeated to me
from memory the whole of what must be regarded
one of the finest productions of his genius—the
verses ending with the refrain " Barbara " (which,

by the way, was the real Christian name of this
unfortunate lady), which occur in the poem " Har-
ton " in the volume of " City Poems." The man is
not to be envied who can read that pensive lyric,
and especially its intensely pathetic close, without
tearful emotion. But the effect produced on the
mind by reading it, cannot equal that produced by
hearing it repeated by the poet's own lips, as it
came fresh from his wounded heart. There never
were two things more mutually adapted than
Smith's composition and his voice. No other man
can read his poetry so well as he did himself. I
have often been greatly moved by his voice,
but I never was so overcome by emotion in
reading or listening to any poetic production as I
was that night. Some, on finding this gem in
" City Poems," have instanced it as indicating that
Smith had made considerable progress as a poet
from the time that George Gilfillan had, as they
think too lavishly, praised him, and the " Life
Drama" was published. But the fact is, whether
such progress had been made or not, there is no

proof of it in this case, as these verses to Barbara, whether actually among the pieces shown to Mr. Gilfillan or not I cannot tell, were certainly composed and repeated in my hearing before " A Life Drama " had been thought of by Mr. Smith. It is, indeed, possible that they received some polishing from the time they were repeated to me till they were published, but that is all.   It may be worthy of notice here, further, that this young lady may be regarded as the second of the " fair shapes " of memory celebrated in the " Life Drama."   The following lines clearly refer to her :—

> " One comes shining like a saint,
>   But her face I cannot paint,
>   For mine eyes and blood grow faint.
>
> " Eyes are dimmed as by a tear,
>   Sounds are rushing in mine ear,
>   I feel only she is here ;
>
> " That she laugheth where she stands,
>   That she mocketh with her hands.
>   I am bound in tighter bands."

Smith now occupied a place occasionally in the

poet's corner of the *Glasgow Citizen*, the most literary weekly newspaper of the West of Scotland, under the editorship of James Hedderwick, himself no mean poet ; while Hugh Macdonald, one of our best minor poets, acted as sub-editor. His first appearance in that newspaper was made in July 6th, 1850, in lines " To a Friend," written in the Spenserian stanza, and signed Smith Murray. But the larger lyrics, several of which had already been composed by him, he wisely re-served in MS. for further elaboration, revisal, and publication in a less ephemeral vehicle.

For several years previously he had been an ardent, though not indiscriminate, admirer of the writings of the Rev. George Gilfillan. Everything from the pen of that gifted minister of Dundee was hailed and diligently perused by him ; and on every occasion of his visiting Glasgow as a preacher or lecturer, Smith was certain to be one of his hearers. No man in Scotland wielded at that time so great an influence over young aspiring minds intent on self-culture as

Mr. Gilfillan ; and among others, Smith was attracted to him by his hearty, impartial appreciation of genius, and the bold utterance of his convictions. By his writings in " Hogg's Instructor," " The Eclectic," " The Critic," etc., Smith's mind was in no slight degree stimulated. Several of his earliest friends remember him speaking frequently of two articles, especially, from Gilfillan's pen, which appeared in " Hogg's Instructor," in July, 1845, on " Genius," as containing sentences which greatly quickened his latent faculties, and, to use his own words, " haunted my mind for months." Hence, at length, emboldened by Mr. Gilfillan's commendations of the " Roman," by Sidney Yendys or Dobell, Smith, after consultation with two of his young friends of the Addisonian Society, resolved to submit a selection of his poems to him whom he had so long admired, and from whose writings he had derived so much benefit. Consequently, in April, 1851, he sent a small parcel of MS., accompanied with a modest letter, soliciting criticism and advice, to Dundee. Mr. Gilfillan

happened, however, to be then from home ; and on
his return, finding a great accumulation of MS.
and correspondence awaiting him, Smith's poems,
written in an unfamiliar, boyish, unformed, and
straggling hand, after being hastily glanced at
were laid aside for fuller inspection at a less busy
hour, and, being overlaid, were soon forgot. No
reply to his letter, therefore, came to Glasgow
during a lapse of several weeks, and, as a natural
consequence, the young aspirant of the muses felt
not a little dejected. Still he retained sufficient
confidence in Mr. Gilfillan's kindliness of nature to
hope that lack of courtesy was not the cause of
his disappointment. So, after some delay, he addressed another modest letter of inquiry regarding
the fate of his MS. This brought speedily a reply
which completely dispelled all his fears and doubts.
Mr. Gilfillan had meantime perused the poems
more carefully, and so appreciative, encouraging,
and eulogistic was his response, that Smith was
filled with unwonted joy, incited to increase hope-
fulness, and stirred to greater activity in composi-

tion.   Other poems, at Mr. Gilfillan's desire were
transmitted for his inspection, and a friendly
correspondence commenced between the poet and
the critic.   Thus several months glided away.   At
length came July, with its usual week of vacation,
and again we set out on a pedestrian tour to the
highlands.

To this trip we had given much precogitation,
in choosing our course, fixing its stages, and
acquiring all the information we could regarding
the most important places and objects of interest.

We first of all sailed by steamer, on Saturday
afternoon, to the head of Lochgoil, then walked
through Hell's Glen to Lochfine, and crossed the
ferry to Inverary, where we remained till Monday
morning.   On Sabbath we attended the parish
church, and were both highly pleased with the
preaching of the venerable minister.   On the afternoon we took a quiet walk to the top of the very
picturesque hill of Duniquoich, discoursing on
sundry enigmas of human life.   From the hill top
we had an extensive view of Lochfine and its sur-

rounding scenery; but having formed very high expectations of the prospect to be enjoyed here, we were on the whole rather disappointed. On Monday morning we started by five o'clock on the road to Oban, by Loch Awe and Ben Cruachan. It was a very pleasant morning. The grey mist still lay upon the mountains. Nature had not yet fully awaked. The solemn stillness of the early morn—a stillness broken only by the muffled ripple of the water rills, and the occasional plaintive bleat of sheep awed our spirits, and we walked on in silence through the narrow lonely glen, till we were suddenly startled by a voice or sound, neither of us had ever heard before—Cuckoo, cuckoo! Instantly we stood, and eye met eye with gleam of gladsome surprise, when Cuckoo, cuckoo, again broke the stillness, leaving it more deep and solemn than before. The joy of our hearts was great. Smith has expressed the feeling thus,—

> " Cuckoo, cuckoo, woke somewhere in the light.
> I started at the sound and cried, 'O voice,
> I've heard you often in the poet's page—
> Now in your stony wilds.' "

Indeed he did utter such a sentiment at the time, though not exactly in such measured cadence. Our pause, however, was but for a moment. On we sped. The mists crept up the mountains' sides, and before the rays of the ascending sun soon vanished quite away. Our path sloped upwards, and at length we came upon the spot called 'Burke's view,"—a view of mountainous grandeur, truly and greatly sublime, over which we hung with a long lingering gaze. Loch Awe now lay before and beneath us in its exquisitely solemn beauty. As we approached it we were much struck with its unruffled stillness, lying low amidst the mountains, while the peculiar transparency of its waters, reflecting with marvellous distinctness the mountain's side and overhanging trees, gave us intense delight. Very pleasant was now our way on to the inn of Cladish, near the head of the loch. Here we rested an hour and breakfasted. Then strapping on our knapsacks once more, we pursued our way round the head of the loch till we came upon the foot of Ben Cruachan, towering upwards in massive majesty, and had the ever memorable ruin of Kilchurn Castle near, directly on our left. Sitting down by the roadside, being reluctant to enter the mountain path and leave this most lovely scene,—we took out our small guide-book, and read anew the story of the castle, and long gazing tried to imagine what it was in the days of its glory, till our reverie was dispelled by the sound of wheels, and looking back upon the road we beheld the coach for Oban advancing towards us. We then resolved to make up for the time we had so pleasantly whiled away here, by driving for half a dozen miles upon the coach. Fortunately for us, though not for the proprietor, there were few passengers, and the driver seemed glad of our signal to stop. So, seated near him, we bowled along through the wild pass of Brandir, with the dark waters of the Awe flowing turbulently beneath us on our left; and entertained by the coachman's naive description of places, and narration of local incidents, till we reached Loch Etive. We then left the coach and resumed our true character of pedestrians. The day was now well spent, and walking by the side of the loch we imagined it would be refreshing to have a bath in its waters. So in we went. This proved rather a serious proceeding, however, as, probably being too much fatigued, the cold water had the effect on Smith of producing vomiting, and so thoroughly prostrating his strength that it was with much difficulty we accomplished the remaining ten miles or so of our journey to Oban. There he became worse, and required to lie in bed till next forenoon under medical attendance. It became, consequently, necessary also to abandon the prospect of completing our projected trip, which was to proceed on foot, by the course of the Caledonian canal to Inverness. Hence having rested one day in Oban, we sailed by steamer to Rothesay, and spent the remainder of our vacation time in boating, and making short rambles on the island of Bute. In a day or two Smith was quite well again, and we had a very agreeable time of it on this, " the fairest and most melancholy of all the islands of the

Clyde." The epithet "melancholy," which Smith has bestowed on Bute, is owing to the presence of numerous emaciated invalids, who frequent the island during summer on account of its remarkably salubrious atmosphere. Our favourite walk while here was to Ascog Point, where the finest of all views upon the island may be had. The prospect of the Clyde there is most extensive, varied, and very lovely. Every day were we seated for a while near the grave of Stanley, first actor, then painter, and devout Christian. This is the spot of which Smith writes in " A Boy's Poem"—

> "There was a ruined chapel on the coast,
>   And by it lay a little grassy grave
>   Still as a couching lamb. The people told
>   How years ago a grey-haired, childless man
>   (His name is still remembered by the world),
>   Came to these shores, and lay down there to rest
>   Till the last trumpet's cry."

Though this is most certainly the scene referred to in these lines, the poet did not intend a precise description of it. He has used a poet's licence, and given at least one touch of imaginary colouring by the word "ruined" in the first line : for the little white chapel, or Free church, by the side of which is Stanley's "grassy grave," is by no means a ruin. And though there are the dilapidated remains of a building at a short distance, it bears evidence of having been employed for a very different purpose than a chapel.

CHAPTER VII.

The Bard and his Herald.

" He has lived all his days
With beauty and with grandeur and with power
Unrecognised till now."   (SMITH).

" The listening throng
Applaud the master of the song."   SCOTT.

STIMULATED by correspondence with Mr.
Gilfillan, Smith now devoted his leisure hours
with increased diligence to poetic composition ;
and in the month of October appeared the first
public notice of his poems, in the pages of the
Eclectic, in an article on " Recent Poets," from Mr.
Gilfillan's pen.   In the same month, too, that
reverend critic being in Glasgow, officiating at a
Communion, met Smith by appointment on the
" preaching Monday," as it is called.   On that day

they walked arm in arm along Trongate in friendly
conversation. They thus met and became personally acquainted for the first time. Gilfillan had
brought " The Garden and the Child," " The Page
and the Lady," and other poems submitted to his
judgment, along with him ; but offered to show
them to the late Dr. Nichol, Professor of Astro-
nomy, before returning them. Mr. Smith gladly
availed himself of this offer ; and the professor was
so highly pleased with a perusal of these pieces
that he immediately invited the young author to
his house, where he was frequently afterwards a
visitor and a guest. It was, indeed, a very common thing, during this winter, for Smith to walk
from the warehouse after eight o'clock p.m., down
to Partick, and spend an hour at the Observatory.
Through these visits he became also of course
acquainted with the professor's son, Mr. John
Nichol, then a student, and presently Professor of
English Literature in the University of Glasgow.
Dr. Nichol was thus the first man of literary
eminence with whom Smith became intimate in

Glasgow, and he remained to his death an ardent and steadfast friend.

In reviewing the University Album of this year, Mr. Gilfillan made another laudatory reference to Smith—presenting him before the students as one worthy of their emulation. And Smith having, during winter, sent him some other productions of his poetic genius—particularly a poem entitled "The Old Manor House"—Gilfillan in the following spring wrote a long article in the *Critic,* on "A New Poet in Glasgow," in which he not only gave copious extracts from several of the MSS. before him, but published some of the poems entire. It was a rare, if not altogether unprecedented proceeding for a critic thus to review poems of a living writer which were still only in manuscript, and Mr. Gilfillan accounted for doing so by saying—" His (Smith's) aim is at present partly to get his poetry printed, but principally to work up his way to a situation more congenial to his mind, more worthy of his powers, and allowing him more leisure for his favourite pursuits." And he called earnestly

"specially on Glasgow friends, ever generous and
warm-hearted, to look to it, that they neglect not
one of the finest poets—perhaps, indeed, one promising to be the finest since Campbell—their good
city had produced."

These notices created a very considerable sensation in the literary world.   The extracts were
generally accepted at the time as verifying the
commendations of the Dundee critic; and the
reading public were not only prepared to welcome
the coming poet, but ardent in expectation of his
first volume.   Seldom, indeed, has any work been
waited for as the " Life Drama " was.   The service
which Mr. Gilfillan thus rendered Smith in heralding his advent into the sacred circle of literature,
and preparing the public for his audience, was very
great.   In one day, and before he had himself
published anything but a few short pieces in the
Glasgow Citizen, Smith had become famous, and
talked of as the new and genuine poet in every
literary club and *coterie* in the kingdom. Letters of
congratulation, from entire strangers, and distant

places, began to flow in upon him. Some ardent
lovers of letters even undertook long journeys in
order to see and encourage him. Thus several
valuable friendships were then formed by him for
life. Among these friendships, not the least note-
worthy was that of Mr. Daniel Lawson, Glasgow.
That gentleman, immediately after the appearance
of Mr. Gilfillan's notices in the *Critic*, procured for
himself copies of these, which he circulated in the
city among persons likely to be interested in, and
of service to, the young struggling bard. He also
sought out Smith, formed a personal acquaintance
with him, and invited him to his house, which became for him during his future residence in Glasgow almost a second home. About this time, also,
I had the pleasure, through a friend intimate with
Hugh Macdonald, of securing Smith's introduction
to that gifted, most genial, and somewhat eccentric
man ; and a very close, endeared, and lasting
friendship was immediately formed between them.
Through Macdonald he was next introduced to
James Hedderwich, Esq., editor of the *Citizen*, who

shortly after introduced him to Mr. Patrick Proctor Alexander, at that time a frequent contributor to the *Citizen* and other Glasgow newspapers, and who became Smith's biographer and editor of " Last Leaves."

As it was towards the close of 1851 that he formed acquaintance with these literary men of Glasgow, and as he removed to Edinburgh at the beginning of 1854, their educational influence upon him was both late and brief.　They may have helped to perfect the poet, but they cannot be regarded as having aided in the making of him.　He was, therefore, to a greater extent than some seem disposed to admit, a truly self-taught man, enjoying only the most meagre advantages of schools and of society in his youth, and indeed till the time at which he became an author.

The truth is, his great teacher, as in the case of every genuine poet, was Nature.　He was educated by her far more than by either men or books.　She was his first teacher and his best.　His works give evidence of this in various ways.

His chief characteristic, alike in verse and prose, is that of literary painter from actual nature. He cannot be said properly to be dramatic : nor is he to any great extent philosophical—in fact, he often spake, at least, so disparagingly of mental philosophy, as rather reflected disadvantageously upon himself. At the same time, he frequently manifested, even in his earliest works, no mean power of mental and moral analysis. But he did so only in brief, though often subtle and beautiful, gleams of genius. In sustained analysis of mind and character he rather failed. He struggled, however, after attaining this power, and so successfully, too, as indicated that, had his life been prolonged he might have possessed it in large measure. But after all, it is analogical rather than in analytical power that he excels. Two things indeed he could do well—depict nature and interpret nature ; but it must be nature in the individual and minute, not in the whole and the comprehensive or complex. These, in truth, he could do as few poets have done. As was truly said in a notice of his earliest works, " No poet that has ever lived has excelled Smith in the beauty and exquisite analogical perception displayed in his images from nature." The individual man, too, he could often well depict, but it was by, as with a glance of intuition, discerning his differential attribute, or distinguishing characteristic. In short, what he most excels in is, scenic description and individual portraiture. His scenes and portraits, however, are almost never imaginary ones—they are pictures from life. His best pieces and passages are those which were written under the inspiration of thought brooding over objects of actual and immediate vision. What he has derived from the inspiration of friends and books, is ever tame compared with what his own excogitation brought him, when gazing with " the faculty Divine " upon the world of human and physical phenomena. Let any thoughtful reader put his works to the test, and he cannot fail to be convinced of this. Let him contrast, for instance, " Edwin of Deira " with " City Poems." In the former, he draws inspiration more from book-world and the distant past ; in the latter, from the world actually before him ; and notwithstanding all the higher polish and poetic finish of the versification of Edwin, it not only lacks the fire and richness, but further, does not possess the heart, soul, and rounded wholeness of some of the poems in the earlier volume. Most assuredly, had " Edwin of Deira " been Smith's first work, he would not on its merits, great as they are, have been received by the public as he was ; and we venture to predict, in opposition to the judgment of some eminent critics, it will not live in the memories of men, and be quoted from in future, as his other and earlier productions. Thus will it be shown that those friends who endeavoured to divert him from the early and natural bent of his poetic spirit which produced his first poems, committed a grave mistake.

What, under changed circumstances and new monitors, and with approved modern models set before him, he gained in classical correctness, would almost seem to have been at the cost of losing a

K

measure of naturalness and originality. One of the chief poetic tendencies of our day is to regard refinement too much. Naturalness is too often enervated and force lost in finish. Over-refining is effeminating. And Smith at first gave promise of heralding a new era in poetry, or at least of initiating a return to a more Burns-like robustness of tone and treatment. Many deeming they saw, amidst all the extravagances of "A Life Drama," indications of this, heartily hailed his advent as a poet. And it would, perhaps, have been better for his fame, had his muse, purged of the follies of its youth, fulfilled that promise. His place in the literature of the age would then have been more distinctly defined, and his influence upon it more potent even than it is.

But to return to our narrative. Smith, knowing that the public—now prepared by the extracts which had been laid before them—awaited the appearance of his poems in their full form, devoted every available moment to preparation for publication. Mr. Gilfillan had suggested to him, however,

that the select literary world would be best satisfied with some longer poem than any he had yet
written, in which the sustained concentration of
his powers might be shown ; and at once he
perceived the justness of the suggestion. But as
no subject for such an effort had yet occurred to
his mind, he began to entertain the thought of
attempting to fuse the detached pieces he had
already composed into one extensive mould,
formed after the plan of one of them, entitled " A
Life Fragment," the first draught of which, from
his own pen, I have in my possession ; while a
second improved and slightly extended copy
was among the papers sent for inspection to Gilfillan. This was to become, when thus expanded,
" A Life Drama." It was, indeed, a difficult and
hazardous conception this to work out. It could
not but prove so far a failure. It was almost a
necessity that it should bear, more or less, traces of
being a patch-work ; and the originally detached
lyrics could not but suffer much in their intrinsic
value by the process of fusion. When he first

mentioned to me this design, I strongly advised him against its prosecution, although I had great confidence in his powers of adaptation. Mr. Gilfillan also expressed doubt of the feasibility of the project. Nothing could prevent him, however, from making the venture. The plot—so far as there is any in "A Life Drama"—was soon formed in outline ; and he immediately proceeded with the work of detaching, transposing, piecing, uniting, and supplementing, with great toil, patience, care, and ingenuity. As the work advanced, and he rehearsed it stage by stage in our walks, I became more and more astonished at his ability and fertility of thought, It was thus "A Life Drama" took shape and development. Was it done at a dash ? No, verily.

> " The full faced moon,
> Set round with stars, in at the casement looked,
> And saw him write and write ; and when the moon
> Was waning dim upon the edge of morn,
> Still sat he writing, thoughtful-eyed and pale."
>
> *   *   *   *   *   *
>
> Great joy he had ; for thought came glad and thick,
> As leaves upon a tree at primrose time ;

> And as he wrote, his task the lovelier grew,
> Like April unto May, or as a child,
> A smile in the lap of life, by fine degrees
> Orbs to a maiden, walking with meek eyes
> In atmosphere of beauty round her breathed.
> *He wrote all winter* in an olden room
> Hallowed with glooms and books."

And summer, too, had come and gone before his task was done.

These facts regarding the history of Mr. Smith's first published poem are not generally known, but they account in great measure for the chief defects and blemishes of the work. They have also an important bearing on the literary character and acumen of the Rev. G. Gilfillan.

Some writers have very broadly charged him with over-praising " *A Life Drama* " in the pages of the *Eclectic* and *Critic*, and so encouraging rather than correcting the spasmodic spirit of the young author. The sins and follies of that work, therefore, whatever they may be, are often thus to some extent rolled and made to lie at his door. But these writers, among whom Aytoun cannot be exempted, have done this either in ignorance of, or by, more or less culpably, ignoring the above facts. The real truth is, when Gilfillan wrote in these magazines heralding a new poet, he had never either seen or heard of "A Life Drama," and could not consequently write about *it.* That work had not then been written; nay, as a work, the chaos of its creation had not come in the poet's mind. They were a collection of short and, all except one, complete poems, that were subjected to Mr. Gilfillan's verdict, and lay before him in MS. when he wrote to these magazines. And, as has been said above, he rather discouraged than otherwise their fusion into one whole. It is not consequently just to accuse him, as has too often been done, of having then and there almost unqualifiedly eulogised "A Life Drama." Indeed to one who knows, and at the time knew intimately all the facts of the case, the criticisms that have often been made on Gilfillan's early notices of Smith, appear to constitute one of the most unreasonable passages in the history of modern literature. It is really wonderful how it all arose. Possibly, however, the oracles of literature may sometimes be thus generally led astray by following too implicity some first voice that sounds from the temple. But the fact is indisputable that Alexander Smith owed more as a literary man, and specially as a poet, to George Gilfillan than to all others. It is certain, too, that Smith thought so himself, and once readily confessed it, whatever reticence he may have maintained when moving in circles in which it had become fashionable to depreciate whatever came from the Dundee critic. And eulogistically as Gilfillan wrote of the poet in his youth, all judges do and must allow, that Smith's after career more than verified the predictions of his enthusiastic herald.

But before his first volume was ready for the press, the month of July came round, and with it his week of holidays. So the MS. was locked up in his desk, and we started on another tour through the highlands. On this occasion we

went, first by train to Dundee, where he called
on the Rev. Mr. Gilfillan, and had an hour's
consultation with him. Thence we proceeded the
same afternoon to Perth, and next morning commenced our pedestrian tour. Our course was
by Crieff, Comrie, and Loch Earn; thence west-
ward by Loch Lubnaig to Callander, and home-
ward, still on foot, to Stirling, where we took train
to Glasgow.

In the meantime, also, he had formed acquaintance with a young lady who became another,
and the last celebrated by him, of the "fair
shapes," who in after-years floated "through the
gardens of his memory;" and regarding whom,
he shortly after being introduced to her, wrote
to me thus :—

" —— is decidedly the cleverest girl I have met
with. I have seen her harpoon that blundering
booby D—— with a lance of wit, in fine style.
She often says fine things in conversation; is a
capital hand at a compliment, as, for instance :
D—— had spoken to her of me as a poet ! and

as such I was introduced. I wrote her two sonnets. A few nights after, I met her, and we had
a walk. She inquired when I intended to
publish; I said something of not being ambitious
of seeing my productions line portmanteaus; she
said, 'Not portmanteaus—they would line memories.' Ye gods, my strong imagination felt a
crown dropping upon my head!

"I have got on pretty well to day;—got a
partner; commenced my speech, and got my
annual dose of cold—a severe one this time.
This cursed weather has done it, and Cardinal
Wiseman is the cause of this darkness—confound
him.

"I think I repeated one of the sonnets I speak
of, to you, up Clyde side. Here is the other :—

> " Our yearning hearts are deeper than our souls,
>   And love, than knowledge, is diviner food ;
>   Though with dead hopes life's rugged paths are strewed ;
>   Though in our ears the muffled death-bell tolls ;
>   And through the silent streets the black hearse rolls ;
>   Yet, the young flowers are laughing in the wood—
>   Where the green linnet feeds her nested brood ;

Yet, rosy children sport on primrose knolls—
Far heard o'er summer leas are summer birds,
And so 'tis in my spirit's dismalness ;
Love is a brightness, that will ne'er depart :
Thine image sleepeth in my soul's caress,
Like a sweet thought within a poet's heart
Ere it is born in joy and golden words.

"I hope you will excuse this scrawl. The fact is I do not feel very well—have no books to read, and two hours to kill.

"I am, most truly yours,

"A. SMITH."

For this young lady Smith entertained much admiration. He came to regret, however, that his acquaintance with her had occasioned her to cherish towards him a tenderer passion than he could reciprocate—a regret not untinged by sorrowful reflections that he had perhaps given her cause for cherishing that passion. And it may, indeed, be regarded as probable that he was working upon his own sombre and wavering experiences in connection with this episode of love, when he wrote "Squire Maurice," one of his finest productions. Through some of even his later poetic effusions also, there runs a note of reminiscent sadness which may not have been wholly artistic or merely fictitious. He was of too noble a nature to forget, or soon cease to mourn the wound he may have, however inadvertently, inflicted on a gentle and over-susceptive young heart.

CHAPTER VIII.

𝔄 𝔏𝔦𝔣𝔢 𝔇𝔯𝔞𝔪𝔞: 𝔦𝔱𝔰 ℭ𝔯𝔦𝔱𝔦𝔠𝔰, 𝔱𝔥𝔢 𝔓𝔲𝔟𝔩𝔦𝔠 𝔞𝔫𝔡 𝔓𝔬𝔢𝔱.

" For me, thus nurtured, dost thou ask
   The classic poet's well-conned task ? "

" Approach those masters, o'er whose tomb
   Immortal laurels ever bloom :
   Instructive of the feebler bard,
   Still from the grave their voice is heard ;
   From them, and from the paths they showed
   Choose honoured guide and practised road."
                                        SCOTT.

SMITH having accepted a generous offer made
to him by Bogue, the publisher, was now busy
supplying copy to the press and correcting proof.
And at length, at the close of the year 1852, his
first book, dated 1853, appeared and created a wide
and profound sensation.

" That was a hit !
   The world is murmuring like a hive of bees—
   He is its theme."

Newspapers, magazines, and reviews were all canvassing its merits. Of praise there was no lack, from some, indeed, no limit ; but adverse criticism was not altogether withheld. To revise, however, the judgments of the *Eclectic*, *Critic*, *Leader*, *Athenæum*, and the quarterlies, is beyond the province of these pages—they are devoted to the life, rather than to the writings of the poet.

Smith had now indeed acquired fame, perhaps by this first work too much fame—more than the work deserved on its real merits; though these were, as must ever be confessed, great, and more than could easily be in future sustained by the author. From the first, he and his most intimate friends perceived and felt this ; indeed, the rapid sale of the book, and the laudations of the many critics, awakened expectations that caused him to join trembling with his mirth. He would have been more than satisfied, he often confessed, with earning a little less fame from his first work ; for while he did earnestly

> " Strive for the poet's crown, he ne'er forgot
> How poor are fancy's blooms to thoughtful fruits ;

That gold and crimson mornings, though more bright
Than soft blue days, are scarcely half their worth."

Besides, no one was more conscious of the defects and blemishes of " A Life Drama " than himself. Before it was out of the press, indeed, his own taste and judgment had condemned much of it ; and greatly did he marvel often at the unmingled praise bestowed on it by some of its critics. The book was the too rapid product of a sensitive mind under the heat of unnatural and unhealthy excitement, which several things had combined to effect. He had been cradled amidst political agitation. His youth had been passed in the very focus of Scottish chartism. In 1848 occurred the last French revolution, and the reflux of that movement had been felt in this country, as was manifest in riotous risings in various parts of the kingdom, but especially in Glasgow. There the mob had at mid-day broken into shops in the very centre of the city ; the military had been called out ; and armed pensioners, too prompt to obey a hasty command, had fired upon the people, fatally shedding blood, which awakened the feeling of revenge in some, and alarm in all ; so that the whole of the inhabitants were thrown for days into a state of ferment. And Smith had been a spectator of the most notable of these riots.

No thoughtful and sensitive young man could be altogether unmoved or uninfluenced in spirit by the political agitations of those days. He was no politician, however, and still less was he a chartist. And with all his poetic sensitiveness, he was as little affected by these circumstances and events, as any one could be. Indeed, by 1848 his life was being spent very much beyond the sphere of politics. He was now living, as far as the sterner necessities of his lot would allow, in a dreamland of poesy, to which he had been lured, and where his spirit was being entranced by voices, among which that of Keats took the lead. And the riotous voices of the ruder world around, bursting violently in upon this poetic region, seemed only to disturb him, and engage his attention for a passing moment. The deep currents of his mind were scarcely touched by the boisterous political events of the time. These never moved him to write one political stanza, even though he had taken to the reading of Ebenezer Elliott. The fact of his doing so may seem contradictory of all this ; but the fact is, it was Elliott's strains of genuine poetry, and not his politics nor patriotism that fascinated Smith.

But a stronger cause of unrest of spirit consisted in his own present and prospective circumstances. He was engaged in an employment uncongenial to his mind ; had ardent longings after a more literary life ; was feeling often the disadvantage of a defective education ; was necessitated to prosecute his favourite studies under this disadvantage, and also "cabined, cribbed, confined," from want of means and leisure ; with little or no visible prospect, too, of bettering his circumstances ; and having no one of influence among his relatives or friends to whom he could look for help or guidance. In such circumstances it was not wonderful that, patient as he was, his spirit should sometimes become despondent, fretful, and irritated.

Then, lastly and chiefly, there came so suddenly upon him that great burst of praise, by means of Mr. Gilfillan's article in the *Eclectic.* That first blare of fame could not but produce, on the mind of so young a man, an excitement, for awhile, unfavourable for the conception and execution of a great poem. But unfortunately, it was precisely at this time that the plan of "A Life Drama" was conceived, concocted, and executed.

And further, while the circumstances of its origin were such, the directing influences of the moment were, unhappily, even more unpropitious. Keats was no longer now the chief controlling spirit of his genius. The spell of Bailey's "Festus," rather, was now upon him. And too much under his influence, it is to be feared, the composition of the work was commenced and carried out. Evidence of this is very apparent when one compares "A Life Drama," with the previously written "Life Fragment," of which it was to some extent an

L

expansion. The latter is throughout in conception, spirit, and treatment, far more Keatsean,—quiet, hazy, dreamy. It is a very different spirit which animates "A Life Drama." The mind of Smith, in fact, was never in such an abnormal state as went he wrote that work. Hence is it that it is so unlike his other works, unlike the man himself, and reflects his own spirit less than anything else that he has written. Every one after reading it felt, in coming into personal contact with the author for the first time, a shock of pleasant surprise; and no wonder. As he has said himself in his fragmentary poem on "Edinburgh," he sung them "urged by passionate unrest." In this state of mind, then, the poem was too hastily conceived, then, by far too hurriedly written during the nights of 1852, and next, too quickly sent to the press. This is the real cause of its imperfections. Before it was quite finished, its author had himself begun to see its unnatural feverishness, and other faults; but the public had been promised, and was waiting for the book; and so it required to go before the world, ere he had time to perfect it by calm reflective thought. And it is almost certain that had it lain for a few months in manuscript in Mr. Smith's desk, for reconsideration, it would never have been presented to the public as it is; much of it would have been recast, and much of it pruned. But written as it was, the chief wonder connected with it is, that it is what it is. Very few indeed could, at his age, in such circumstances, and after such a fashion produce a work equal to it. It is a marvellous production, and a knowledge of all the facts relating to its composition only tends to make it appear more marvellous. The fame it brought him was great, but it was well merited, and undoubtedly it was by him much prized. But that fame was also perilous to a young beginner in authorship. To be raised so high so suddenly, however sweet to the poet, was to the man—ay, and to the poet, too, of necessity trying.

Smith, however, bore the ordeal with a magnanimity rare at any age, but doubly rare in youth;

which disarmed envy, won the admiration of all
around him, and evinced that the man was even
greater than the poet. Few have ever walked
forth from being crowned with such a wreath of
laurels, with a heart so little changed, and as meek
and manly a bearing, as he did. In fact, few with
a poetic temperament could do so. To his fellow-
workmen, acquaintances, and friends, he was the
same as ever. His fame turned other heads : his
own it never turned.

It was at once amusing and pitiable to see, day
after day, some lackadaisical-looking youths standing at the warehouse-door at four or eight o'clock
p.m., to get a glimpse of the poet as he came out,
and to hear the whisperings—" There he's, there
he's " !—whisperings which he sometimes heard,
and was wont to hitch his shoulders, muttering
an " Uh !" as, after hurried steps behind him, and
he was immediately the object of a not very
polite stare. But there were others than in-
discreet youths who half amused and half annoyed
him.

He was now invited frequently to dinner and evening parties by persons of good position in society, and men of literary taste. But to be lionised, however sweet it may be, and generally is, especially to talented young men, he not only had no liking for, but felt a very positive aversion to it ; while against the dissipating influences of the festive board, which have proved so irresistible and destructive to many of the sensitive sons of genius, he stood watchful and invincible. Some of those to whose table he was invited, and several whom he met there as fellow guests, desired to know how they might be helpful in procuring for him a situation more congenial to his mind than that he was presently still engaged in. And Smith was wont to relate, with much humorous enjoyment, that on one such occasion, a wealthy paterfamilias asked him into a private room, and after questioning him regarding the kind of situation he would like, said he was a believer in phrenology, understood the science perfectly, and desired Smith to permit him to manipulate his head, being confident that he would thereby discover what trade or profession would best suit and be most profitable to him. This request being granted, and the poet's head having been scientifically examined with great care, the phrenologistic old gentleman, assuming a wise and patronising air, seriously advised his young friend to give up all idea immediately of prosecuting poetry or literature as a profession, as the fates were dead against him in these paths. He would not, he could not, succeed in either. He had been endowed for another kind of life altogether ; in fact, he was constituted phrenologically for trading in dry goods, and, according to his best judgment, the business of a drysalter would suit him better than any other : and as he had influence with one of the chief houses in that trade, he had no doubt that he could soon procure him a situation as learner there. Smith had only to signify acquiescence, and he would see about it at once. But Smith, seeing that the generous old gentleman was riding a hobby, with expressions of thanks for so much kindliness of intention, re-

quested a day or two to think of the matter, and
so escaped.

As illustrative of the general fame of the young
poet in the city at this time, one incident of an
amusing nature may be given. A rather popular
preacher in the east of Glasgow, being informed
by one of his congregation that Alexander Smith,
"the new poet of Glasgow," had of late been
several times a hearer at his evening sermons, felt
not a little elated, and began to think there must
be more in his preaching than in his humility
he had himself imagined, seeing it could attract
such a man of genius. But, alas, on making
further inquiry, he learned, to his mortification,
that the attraction was not the preacher in the
pulpit, but a tradesman's pretty daughter in one
of the pews. On this discovery the reverend
gentleman used no more efforts to form personal
acquaintance with the poet.

"The new Glasgow Poet," or "the Poet of
Glasgow," were titles now frequently applied to
him, but which he very much disliked to hear or

read. One of the most respectable and extensive
booksellers of the city, whose shop was near to
the warehouse in which Smith wrought, on receiv-
ing the first parcel of " A Life Drama," advertised
it by a large handbill in his window, as " A. Life
Drama, by Alexander Smith, the Glasgow Poet,"
and Smith's eye falling on the announcement as
he went to his work, his modesty was so stung,
that he immediately sent a courteous note, re-
questing the placard to be, as a favour, removed,
seeing he made no pretensions to the character it
ascribed to him ; and the offensive notice instantly
disappeared.

The chief and almost only difference observable
in his manner of life from the time that he became
known to the public, consisted in his mode of
spending the Sabbath. Up till that time he had
been a very regular attender of public worship
on that day ; but now his Sabbaths were most
frequently passed altogether apart from the church.
Fidelity to truth demands this fact to be recorded.
The auses however, of his being now more fre-

quently than previously "with nature on the Sabbath day," it is not so easy to assign. But this much is certain, the change was not the consequence of the abandonment of any religious conviction. It was merely a defection in practice, not in principle, and consequently one which he would not himself defend. It was observable at the time, and is noticed here, because he was from early youth of a religious temperament. It was certainly from religious feeling, awakened in him apparently by painful events recorded near the beginning of this memoir, that he was induced to entertain thoughts of entering the Christian ministry. That purpose was his own; and not merely the fond fancy of partial parents to see their clever boy some day "wag his head in a pu'pit." He was, however, always of a reserved disposition regarding personal religious life and experience. In our more private and confidential moments of conversation, notwithstanding, he became occasionally communicative respecting this hidden life ; and often showed that the great

truths of Divine revelation had touched the centre
of his soul and awakened within him both thought
and feeling.　He was ever, moreover, of a reveren-
tial spirit.　No one ever heard him jest or talk
lightly on religious subjects; nor could he enjoy
or tolerate such levity in others.　His mind was
also richly imbued with Bible-truth; and his
highest early poetic aspirations inclined towards
working some of the historic characters of the
sacred volume into an epic or dramatic poem.
At the time he was engaged, for example, writing
"A Life Fragment,"—one of his earliest pieces,—
begun about his nineteenth year, and which formed
the germ of "A Life Drama,"—although the fruit
proved very unlike the bud—he was also, from a
poetic standpoint, pondering the Life of Moses;
and on several occasions spake of it as affording
peculiarly rich material for a great epic; expressed
his surprise at no one having attempted it, and
his hope of being able himself some day to treat
it in a worthy manner.　When asked whether he
had made any commencement of such a work,

he answered, No—it was a subject far too high
above his reach presently; would require greater
maturity of mind than he now possessed, and
would after all demand years of study: but he
meant to keep it before him. His ideal poet, too,
at that time certainly was

"One who should hallow poetry to God."

When he wrote so regarding the poet who

"Must ere long arise
And with a regal song sun-crown this age,"

he wrote as his heart felt, his spirit prompted, and
his mind approved. Indeed, his religiousness of
spirit in those days reflected itself in his verse to
an extent that his works do not now indicate. In
"A Life Drama"—by no means the product of
a genuine inspiration, but rather of an impulse
suddenly kindled by "strange fire," through reading such works as Bailey's "Festus"—his poetic
soul rushed almost wildly through a new and
foreign channel; and he became unfortunately so
far liable to be misjudged, by many, for this his

first book. Several of the poems of which that work was composed were of a truly religious tone. One such, and among the first written, entitled "The Consecration," containing the song of Earth's history, lies before me in MS., which though neither after the manner of Milton, nor Young, nor Cowper, nor Watts, nor Montgomery, breathes a truly religious spirit. And here is another piece of those days, which I extract from a letter, not doubting that the judicious and generous will pardon any juvenilities discernible in it, in consideration of its being written about his nineteenth year, and also of its general character and worth. It is hardly needful to premise that it is addressed to a student of theology.

"O thou of thoughtful brow and daring heart,
  Speed on thy lofty path like feathered dart ;
Who can withstand the siren voice of fame,
Nor bend in worship to that shade—A name :
Follow the promptings of thy burning soul,
Sweep like a tempest to that distant goal ;
Toil on, thou noble heart—nor let despair
Unnerve thy soul ; but nobly, boldly dare—

Dare with thine arm to bear the Cross unfurled,
And gather, 'neath its ample folds—a world.
This be thy task : what though no marble tomb
In gloomy grandeur frowns o'er thy long home !
If not a leading star in Fame's bright van,
Know this—the first was ne'er the noblest man,
The world's best blood was not a blazing sun,
His life was unrevered ; his grave unknown.
Prove not a traitor to thy sacred trust
Through love of life, nor passion, nor the lust
Of gold.   Fight well, thou warrior of God,
And cleave a path to heaven's bright abode—
Return with garlands from the holy war,
Then shine beyond the sky a meteor star."

But even the "Life Drama" itself contains not a few indications of the more religious spirit of those earlier poems out of which it was compiled.   Besides the passage on the "poet who should ere long arise," already referred to, that other on the degradation of the human soul (pages 28—35), may be instanced, with the remark that the part containing a turbid love passion did not exist in the original. What could be finer, after the "wail" of the preceding lines, than this—

"Brothers, hush ! the Lord Christ's hands
Ev'n now are stretched in blessing o'er the sea and o'er the lands."

And the close too—

> "Lo ! I see long blissful ages, when these mammon days are done,
> Stretching like a golden ev'ning forward to the setting sun."

Mark, also, how, at the close of " A Life Drama,"
the hero emerging at length out of the whirlpool
of passion in which he "tore at all the creeds,"
confesses to his friend thus—

> " *Charles.*   He told me once,
> The saddest thing that can befall a soul,
> Is when it loses faith in God and woman ;
> For he had lost them both—Lost I those gems—
> Though the world's throne stood empty in my path,
> I would go wandering back into my childhood,
> Searching for them with tears.

> " *Edward.*   Let him go
> Alone upon his waste and dreary road,
> He will return to the old faith he learned
> Beside his mother's knee.   That memory
> That haunts him, as the sweet and gracious moon
> Haunts the poor outcast earth, will lead him back
> To happiness and God."

And as if the poet himself were returning to the
purer and truer purpose of his earlier youth, he
closes the book with the noble sentiment—

"I will go forth 'mong men, not mailed in scorn,
　But in the armour of a pure intent.
　Great duties are before me, and great songs ;
　And whether crowned or crownless, when I fall,
　It matters not, so as God's work is done.
　I've learned to prize the quiet lightning-deed,
　Not the applauding thunder at its heels,
　Which men call Fame."

He that could even think that thought,—the man who could write these noble lines, must have had something truly noble, genuinely Christian in his spirit. And let it be remembered that these fine and truly religious passages are fragments of his earliest poems.

That he was ever, however, even in his earliest years, what is commonly understood by the phrase "a religious poet," is not here meant to be asserted. All that is maintained is, that he was truly religious in spirit. The sensuousness even, or as some think and have said, the super-sensuousness of "A Life Drama," did not characterize those poems which he submitted to the critical eye of the Rev. George Gilfillan. They were free from that, perhaps the chief, fault of that work. And though after its publication he did " proceed to veil the statue of the Venus, and to uncover those of the Apollo and Jupiter," my opinion, formed from long and close intercourse with him, is that his early religiousness of poetic spirit suffered partial decadence for a time, from want of depth of religious thought, and that owing to a combination of causes. First of all, in part, from personal idiosyncrasy.

Naturally, instinctively he shrank from any process of lengthened logical analysis, or abstruse scientific investigation. He did not really seem to dislike religious science more than he did all mental science ; nor religious disputation more than political disputation ; but he disliked them all, and, that apparently very much alike. Indeed, he not inaptly describes himself, when in his essay on " Books and Gardens," he makes " the doctor " say, " There is no use speaking on such matters to our incurious, solitary friend here, who could bask comfortably in sunshine for a century, without once inquiring whence came the light and the heat."* He was therefore always more likely to shirk than to fight " the spectres of the mind "—to avoid them than to lay them. In short, he was born more a poet than a philosopher. The strongest propension of his mind was to poetry, not in any true sense to philosophy. The greatest of poets, indeed, are precisely those who have been most philosophic. And here from the first was the rock of peril in Smith's path : in order that he might rise to one of the highest seats in the temple of song, he required to overcome a natural aversion to deep scientific thinking on mental and moral truth, and a too great readiness to be satisfied with beauty merely, mainly, or *per se.*

But—and as a second causative—in his early education he had no guide or adviser, and so was left to follow too freely his own impulses, which being followed become always more dominant. True mental discipline, such as may be gained in college life, he had not received. And the time available, in his adolescent age, for mental self-

* "Dreamthorp," page 265.

M

culture, was hardly sufficient even for the gratification of his strong poetic tendencies.

As he advanced in life, however, he seems to have felt progressively the need of philosophic thought in loftiest song, and so—

"Another and a nobler me"

was rising within him ; and he was evidently in his later years looking into the arena of truth, and equipping himself for grappling there with the deeper questions of the human soul, and man's destiny.

Further, being of a gentle and pacific nature, the Church early disappointed and dissatisfied him. The bitter conflicts of creeds, the often rancorous polemics, and acrimonious contentions of the clergy, divines, and theologians, were to him the most "wretched jangling" of all in this poor world. The almost incessant internal war-cries and actual wars of the Church,—which ought to have been the choicest sphere of concord, rest, and peace,—appeared to him to indicate that there was no rest to be found by entering her pale, and he became evermore disposed to stand apart from her, as from an arena of discord. Alas! how many such gifted, sensitive, thoughtful, and specially poetic minds; how many of naturally the finest spirits of our country, have during this and past ages been repelled from the visible Church from the same cause!

But once more, unfortunately, the spirit of his first book, constrained the more strictly religious world to look askance upon him as a poet. The learned men of the Church, her ministers, and journalists failed, therefore, to hail and countenance him as heartily as others did, and he became through contact with kindred spirits a poet of the times. And here we come upon a fourth source of moulding or directing influence—the current poetic spirit of our age. It is not wonderful that in his early circumstances, at least, he should have been, in a large measure, influenced by that spirit. It is not in the loftiest sense a thoughtful one—not at any rate a thoughtfully religious one. We have hymn writers in abundance, and a few good ones;

but no poet of our day has manifested any great depth of sound religious thought. The most eminent perhaps, is Keble; but even he was after all only the most exquisite of hymnologists. In Tennyson's "In Memoriam" too, "that strain I heard was of a higher mood" than is common with other poets of our period. The poets and strictly literary men of our day have too generally devoted themselves merely, at best, to the æsthetics of religion. Theirs is the religion of sentiment oftener than that of strong sound sense; of the imagination or fancy rather than of the intellect; of the heart rather than of the head,—indeed sometimes as divorced from the head. Feeble are the hands that now essay to strike the harp of Milton, and feeble are the notes, which they evoke. It still waits the master spirit who shall wake its melody as of old. Smith was cast among men of another mould, and almost, and no marvel in so young a man, became one of them. It is to the credit, too, of the Rev. George Gilfillan that he early saw Smith's danger here,

and as he had been the first encourager of his
muse, he was now the first to warn him; when,
soon after the publication of "A Life Drama,"
sketching him in his "Gallery of Literary
Portraits," he wrote thus:—"Now here we think
is the vital defect of the poem (A Life Drama),
the one thing which prevents us applying to it the
epithet 'great.' Mr. Smith is no infidel, and his
poetry breathes at times an earnest spirit, but
his views on such subjects are extremely vague
and unformed. He does not seem sufficiently
impressed with the conviction that, no poem ever
has deserved the name of great, when not impreg-
nated with religion, and when not rising into
worship. His creed seems too much that of
Keats, 'Beauty is truth—truth beauty.' We repeat
that he should look back to the past, and think
what are the poems which have come down to us
from it, most deeply stamped with the approba-
tion of mankind, and which appear most likely to see
and glorify the ages of the future. Are they not
those which have been penetrated and inspired by

moral purpose, and warmed by religious feeling ? We speak not of sectarian song, nor of the common generation of hymns and hymn writers ; but we point to Dante's 'Divina Commedia ;' to all Milton's poems ; to Spenser's 'Fairy Queen ;' to Herbert's 'Temple ;' to Young's 'Night Thoughts ;' to Thomson's 'Seasons ;' to some of the better strains of Pope and Johnson ; to Cowper, to Wordsworth, Southey, and Coleridge. . . . The poet who would not merely shine the meteor of a moment, the stare of fools, and the temporary pet of the public, but would aspire to send his name down, in thunder and music, through the echoing aisles of the future, and become a benevolent and beloved potentate over distant ages, and millions yet unborn, must tread in their footsteps, and seek after the hallowed sources of their inspiration." This was timely and noble advice, to which he doubtless gave heed.

Mr. Smith, then, never, perhaps, possessed any such well defined religious creed as would satisfy the schools of theology. That, however, is in very many instances in this country a possession of no great value. And one may be none the less a true Christian that he is not well versed in all the subtleties of a modern Scottish scribe or Pharisee. But after all, that he was to the close of his life of a genuinely religious spirit, is made abundantly evident by the works of his maturer years; especially by his prose works, and most of all by his essays, as in "Dreamthorp," where we have more of the *inner life* of the author revealed than in his poems. Who, for instance, can read the essays on "Death, and the Fear of Dying," and "Christmas," without regarding their author as writing them under the shadow of the Cross, with a spirit made reverent by contemplation of Him who hung thereon?

And what cause have we to doubt that it was the same religiousness of mind which prompted him in his early youth to think of making Moses the subject of an epic, which induced him, at length, to select as the topic of his last, and his only historic poem, the introduction of Christianity into Britain? Indeed, that also was a subject which had early, and so long, engaged his thoughts—as witness "An Evening at Home," which forms part of his first published volume, and contains what must be regarded as the germ of "Edwin of Deira." Further, a review of his works as a whole, furnishes pleasing indications that, as a writer, he was becoming, through the mellowing influences of years, and increasing realization of life's responsibilities and solemnities, ever more Christian in thought and expression. In fine, though he was no avowed or exemplary churchman, he would fail in more than Christian charity, who would venture to pronounce him other than a sincere Christian.

But let us return from endeavouring to analyse the character of the man, to continue the tracing of the more external events of his history.

From Mr. Bogue he had received £100 for his first book, and with this sum in hand, and a path opened to a literary career, he resolved to leave the trade of designer at the termination of his year's engagement. In the course of a few months this purpose was fulfilled ; and as his father and the rest of the family removed about the same time to Williamsburgh, near Paisley, he took a trip through England towards London, in order to see the country, and form acquaintance with some of the literary men of the capital. On this trip he was accompanied by Mr. John Nichol, and in the course of it I received a number of interesting letters from him, of some of which a few extracts may be given :

> *" Ambleside, Monday evening.*

" MY DEAR B——

"I have seen Liverpool, Ulverston, and Biggs. . . . During the last two days I have been among the lakes. Some of them are nearly as wild, and others more soft and beautiful than anything of the same kind in Scotland. I crossed Barrowdell Pass yesterday—a very hard pull it was, but the view from the head was magnificent. In coming down I really thought I would have broken my neck. . . . I spent some time in Grassmere churchyard. Wordsworth sleeps there, with a number of his friends, and many of the members of his own family around him. The sight is affecting enough. Afterwards, I saw the great poet's sister—the companion of his rambles. She has been crazy for twenty years, is now very old and frail, and when I saw her she was drawn about in a wheeled chair.

"We called on Miss Martineau a few hours ago. No one from her appearance would suspect her of the sin of authorship. She told a melancholy story of 'Jane Eyre,' who is unwell.

     *   *   *   *   *

There is to be a party at Martineau's to-morrow night. Nichol and I are invited, and I suppose must show face. I will be in Halifax on Saturday. Should you find time to drop a few lines for me I would take it kind. Should you do so address to me at the Post Office. Good-night.

          "Yours affectionately,

              "A. SMITH."

"*Oriental Bank Corporation,*

" *Walbrook, London, Saturday morning.*

" Since I wrote you I have seen a considerable
part of England. After finishing the lake country,
we came through a part of Yorkshire, containing
the finest scenery and the stupidest people it has
been my lot to witness. I have seen Bradford,
Halifax, Manchester—where we spent a day with
John Stobes Smith—Sherwood Forest, Nottingham, etc. I met 'Festus' at Nottingham. Although I have modified my opinion of him vastly,
I could not but look upon him with eager interest.
. . . The day after I met him we visited New-
stead Abbey together. . . . I have been a
week in London, and have been enjoying myself
in the best manner I can. Last Saturday I was at
a literary party, and was much amused by a girl
who fastened upon me there. She is a Miss ——
She professed vast admiration for my bridge scene.
Later in the evening she laid me completely on my
back, after this fashion : ' I am going to ask you a
question, Mr. Smith, and you need not answer it

unless you choose, you know. Would it not have been as well to have married Violet and Walter at once, and not have sent them through such a career of sin and misery?' I did not think the time and place was suitable for an explanation, so I parried the question as dexterously as I could. On Wednesday last I drove some forty miles south of London, to dine with Martin F. Tupper, author of 'Proverbial Philosophy.' . . . He lives in a most beautiful part of the country, and gives good dinners: two virtues which I hope will cover his literary sins. I called on Herbert Spencer and Lewes yesterday. Spencer is a quiet, Scotch-looking, thoughtful man. He wishes me to go to the opera with him next week. . . . Lewes and I go to Windsor next Saturday. To-day, Anderson and I go to Buckinghamshire. He returns on Monday, and I go to Yendys' to stay a few days, so I won't be in London till next Tuesday. My new edition appears on Wednesday first. Anderson sends his compliments, and

"I remain, yours affectionately, A. SMITH."

For preparing this new edition of "A Life Drama" for the press he was handsomely remunerated by Mr. Bogue, whose entire conduct towards the young author was most honourable and generous. After paying him the stipulated £100 for the MS., he, before Smith left London, gave him £50 additional as a present, besides a number of valuable books It is to this £50 that Smith refers in the following letter.

London, July 14, 1853.

"MY DEAR BRISBANE,—

"I got yours an hour ago, and very glad was I to get it. I could not think what had kept you silent so long. I have been running about the country a good deal of late. I just returned from M'Dougal this morning, . . . Since I wrote to you I have spent some time at Cheltenham with Yendys. Neither he nor his wife are in good health. His book is to be out in October. I have also been down at Cambridge, and dined in the great hall with the professors and dons.

Very good fellows all of them. I saw a good deal of the person who reviewed me in the *Spectator*, as also the man who worked me off in the *Nonconformist.* I have not seen your brother yet, but mean to try and see him to-morrow. . . I will be in Paisley on Monday first, and will be at your service any time after that you please. I will see you in the course of next week. I got the fifty pounds from Bogue to day. . . . It is amusing to see Hugh (Macdonald) coming out *à la* Gilfillan. The verses *are* good ; but I think, also, he has made rather too much of them. Biggs makes his appearance in the *Critic* on the 18th.

" Yours,

" A. Smith."

In the course of the following week, he called on me as promised in the above letter, and we arranged for a short excursion together to the highlands. Accordingly, in a few days, we went to Aberfoyle, and thence to the Trossachs. As he now resided with his family at Williamsburgh,

we only met about once each week for some time.
He felt too lonely, however, to enjoy residence
in Paisley. His friends were all in Glasgow, and
his visits to the city soon became more frequent.
It was about this time he received an invitation
from the Duke of Argyle to visit him at his castle
at Inverary. In compliance with this invitation,
he spent a week at the ducal palace, and very
much enjoyed the society of his grace, and of
Lord Dufferin, who also happened to be there at the
time, and after his return humorously contrasted
this visit to Inverary with his first, on the occasion
of our second pedestrian trip to the highlands.

His fame had now spread far. An edition of
double the usual number of copies, had been sold
of "A Life Drama" in the course of a few months,
and a second had appeared. Foreign journals
had also made his name favourably known on the
continent ; while in America his book was being
sold in thousands. He now began a literary
career, by undertaking the editorship of a magazine called the *Glasgow Miscellany*, which was

started by Mr. Robert Buchanan, editor of the *Glasgow Sentinel* newspaper, and father of Robert Buchanan the poet. This literary effort, however, like all such undertakings in Glasgow, proved a failure. And on Smith accepting a situation which necessitated his leaving the city, it came suddenly to an end.

CHAPTER IX.

In Edinburgh.

"Thy sons, Edina, social, kind,
With open arms the stranger hail ;
Their views enlarg'd, their lib'ral mind
Above the narrow, rural vale ;
Attentive still to sorrow's wail,
Or modest merit's silent claim :
And never may their sources fail!
And never envy blot their name !"

BURNS.

THE secretaryship of the Edinburgh university, which now became vacant, was just such a situation as Mr. Smith had long desired to occupy : and being encouraged by several of his friends to make application for it, he immediately did so. There was a considerable number of candidates for the office, however ; but having secured the influence of James Hedderwick, Robert Chambers, the Duke of Argyle,

N

and Duncan McLaren—then Lord Provost, and afterwards Member of Parliament for the city,— he became the successful applicant. The post was confessedly conferred on him in consideration of his poetic abilities. He possessed, however, every other qualification necessary for a proper discharge of its duties, and entered the university as its secretary in the beginning of the year 1854. After he had thus settled in Edinburgh we corresponded for a while, almost weekly, in writing. The following extracts from one of his letters at this time give a glimpse of him in beginning life in the Scottish capital.

" Edinburgh.

" MY DEAR TOM,

"I got your welcome letter the other day, and am glad to think there is a chance of your being through here so soon. . . . I feel Edinburgh very dreary occasionally—a sad want of old habits, places, and companions. By my teetotalism there hangs a tale; and a year hence this abstinence will either be the most heroic or the most insane proceeding I ever engaged in.

"Does your next session take place in Edinburgh or Glasgow? I think you mentioned to me some time ago that you thought you might require to come here. I hope it may be so. Did you see 'Festus, a criticism by Murillo,' in 'Hogg'? and what do you think of it? . . . The hint you give at the end of your letter concerning other matters I can understand. Perhaps as far as you are presently concerned it is a pity—perhaps not. We have been comrades and have marched together some eight stages of life's journey with a pretty good knowledge of one another's burdens; and I suspect both of us are now in most precarious circumstances—on the very skirts of the skirmish; and a few years must either bring us success or defeat. Such matters are not so important now as they were a few years ago; but they are matters which letter writing cannot do justice to. Were we on a still hill-side, or on the tramp, with a white road stretching miles before us, or in a gloaming room, with a window opening on the sea, we might talk of such like affairs, but assuredly they are not to be written about. For myself I confess the future makes me often afraid—one sees so much *in* himself to fear, and so much *out* of himself. Remember me to C. and C., and believe me,

" Yours faithfully,

"A. SMITH."

It was my privilege to spend a pleasant week as his guest early in the following summer; and having gone again to Edinburgh in autumn to complete my studies, we had several delightful rambles together to Lasswade, Roslin, and other places around the city, and enjoyed many happy evenings in his lodgings. New and genial friends were gathering around him, and the dreariness of which he had complained shortly after leaving Glasgow, ceased to be felt by him. Sydney Dobell was then residing at Corstorphine, and between the two young poets a close, cordial friendship had commenced. One of my happiest reminiscences of that time is that of accompanying Smith on one occasion to Corstorphine, and being introduced by him to the author of " The Roman," whom we found along with his still delicate, but most amiable wife, gazing with much admiration from the drawing-room window, on a gorgeous sunset. As fruit of this friendship, and these evening visits to Corstorphine, there appeared in the following year, 1855, " War Sonnets," a little volume or poetical *brochure* on the Crimean war, the joint composition of the two friends.

Having at length left Edinburgh on the completion of my studies, we still continued to correspond frequently by letter. There is nothing in that correspondence, however, of more than private interest, till the following was received :—

" December 1st, 1856.

" MY DEAR BRISBANE,

" I got your letter the other day, and was

glad to hear that you had got yourself comfortably located. I expected to see you every
day here; but I then thought that your time
being short you would find at the last you
had ten thousand times too many things to do,
and so just push on to Aberdeenshire. I trust
you will find your new mode of life pleasant,
and exciting enough to keep your blood warm
during the winter.

"The newspaper came with the account of
your ordination. I could hardly help smiling
at the thought that, much has come to both
of us, which, walking about the outskirts of
Glasgow some ten years ago, we looked forward to with great interest, and perhaps some
little doubt; and how much a matter of course
it seems now!

"I don't know if you have seen in the
papers the sudden death of Mr. Bogue, the
publisher. He died about a week ago. I had
a letter just a few days before his death from
him, and it was arranged that I should make

my appearance for the second time in spring. Whether Tilt (his old partner, who is now conducting the business) will publish me, I don't know. I don't apprehend any serious obstacle in the way of getting a publisher.

"I inclose a little poem which I printed in the *National Magazine*, and should be glad to hear what you think of it. I am at present busy with an essay on the Scottish Ballads, for a volume of Edinburgh essays, on the same plan as those volumes issued by the Universities of Cambridge and Oxford. I must have it finished before I leave this for the holidays at Christmas, as the volume is advertised for the second week of January.

"Many thanks for your invitation at Christmas, being the third I have to Aberdeenshire at this moment. To each and all of them I must express my gratitude, and decline. A certain lady from the Hebrides is to be in Glasgow at that time, so I cannot come. If D—— lies on the line of railway from

Inverness, I may perhaps drop in upon you in April. Take a wife, Tom. Now is your opportunity. You have a position, a house, and everything ready.

"There is nothing new here. We have Thackeray lecturing, and Edinburgh crammed itself into the music hall, and *ruffed* and applauded most lustily.

"R—— is still in Edinburgh. He says he does not think he will go forward to the Church at all.

"I suppose you won't be South for some time. Write to me and let me know how you get on.

"Yours faithfully,

"A. SMITH."

But as we were now both busily engaged in the work to which we had respectively devoted ourselves, our correspondence by letter became gradually less frequent; and I had not been favoured with an epistle from him for some considerable time, when the following, which explains itself, came to hand :—

"MY DEAR BRISBANE,

"I know I have acted very badly in not writing earlier ; but for my sin I must plead, in extenuation, a multitude of good intentions and, fortunately, some little business. I have been arranging matters for a certain great event, which has, I confess, knocked all minor things out of my head. The wedding takes place on Monday first. To you and to all other friends of my bachelorhood I wave a farewell, and trust that in that other life I may know you all again.

"I have but little news. I am in press again. This time my publishers are the Macmillans of Cambridge, who give me £250 for the book, the copyright to remain with me. When they make the same amount of profit, the profits are to be equally divided, so that if the thing is at all a success in a commer-

cial point of view, I will gain more by it.   I
expect £100 or £50 from America also.   The
people who printed the 'Life Drama' have
been written on the subject, and I expect an
answer soon.   I think Macmillan's offer extremely liberal ; and taking the time I have
been in Edinburgh, in which the greater portion
of the work has been done, and the little wind-
falls of money for other literary work, . . .
in conjunction with my salary at college, there
is a tolerable prospect that, with thriftiness and
economy, Flora and I will be comfortable enough.

"I can't tell you how strangely I feel in my present circumstances.   Happy, of course ; but happy
with a kind or degree of fear and trembling at the
heart of it that makes it more intense, while it
troubles and shakes it.   What the future is I do
not know ; and I cannot command it.   When a
man is alone, he does not care much : with the
earth beneath his feet, the sky above his head, and
a decent kind of conscience in him, he scrambles
along pretty jollily ; but when another nature is

bound up with his own—who must accept the same fate, whether of bliss or bale, smile in the same sunshine, bow the head to the same storm of driving rain—why it *does* make one feel a little anxious. But hang it !—these ghosts ought to slink into their graves. What have *they* to do showing their empty sides and ugly faces among orange blossoms and the silver voices of the marriage bells ?

"I am sorry that our plans will not allow us to come round by Inverness, so that we shall not have the pleasure of seeing you, as I at one time hoped. We leave Skye on Tuesday by the steamer, and mean to stay a few days at Oban, and reach Edinburgh on Friday or Saturday night. F. has never been at the Trossachs, and I expect great delight in a trip there when the summer session closes ; and I have also a desire to establish myself for some few weeks at Strone or Kilmun. Is there any chance of your being in Edinburgh soon ?— With best wishes, I remain, yours affectionately,

"A. SMITH."

His marriage, referred to in the above letter,

took place in the spring of 1857. The lady to whom he was then united was Miss Flora Macdonald, daughter of Mr. Macdonald, of Ord, Skye, and related in blood to the heroine of that name; and connected also with Horatio Maculloch, the painter, between whom and Smith a very cordial friendship existed.

In the course of little more than a year after his marriage, he removed from Edinburgh to sweet Gesto Villa, at Wardie, near Granton, where on two occasions I had the pleasure of lodging over a night with him.

The above letter also makes reference to the publication of " City Poems " this same year. This, though to discerning readers the best of all Mr. Smith's poetical works, did not meet with such success as his first volume. From various causes the tide of popular sentiment had now ceased to run so strongly in his favour as it had once done. He had been accused of the sin of extensive plagiarism by some, and condemned by others as too sensational.

To the latter charge fullest expression was given in a satirical poem written by Professor Aytoun, and published in 1855, under the title—"Firmilian: a Spasmodic Tragedy, by T. Percy Jones." That work proved a decided hit: it burst like a bomb in the circle of literature, and executed considerable damage on the reputation of several poets. This it did more, perhaps, on the ground of its being well timed, than because of intrinsic poetic worth. It was certainly, however, characterized by great pungency and superlative smartness, in exposing what it termed the "spasmodic" school of poetry to unsparing ridicule. And no one in reading it could fail to perceive that Gilfillan, as a critic, and Bailey, Dobell, and Smith, as poets, were the chief *dramatis personæ;* while Carlyle and Ruskin, as prose writers, did not entirely escape being represented.

Smith was wont to laugh heartily over several passages of this book which most directly referred to himself; always spoke of it as a production of true genius, and never bore any malicious grudge

against its author.   But, at the same time, he did
not altogether enjoy its allusions to himself: indeed,
nó man in his circumstances could do so.   Nothing
so prejudices the mass of men against a public
man or author as, though excessive, deserved, and
so successful, ridicule.   And as this was achieved
in " Firmilian " with superlative cleverness, public
sentiment which had, perhaps, become already
sated with its own over-rapturous applause at
"A Life Drama," began to look shy at its author.

While thus his popularity had commenced to
decline, the other less just, and even less scrupulous
and unmerciful attack upon his fame, told with far
more effect than it would otherwise have done.
The charge of plagiarism could happily be answered with the common weapon of fair argument,
and not a few pens voluntarily fought powerfully
thus in Smith's defence.   While Shirley Brooks, in
a smart characteristic paper in *Punch,* did him,
perhaps, fully as much service as any or all others.
Many generous friends, also, from different quarters,
wrote consolingly and encouragingly to him private

letters of assurance that this was only a passing cloud of infamy which would soon pass away.

The ridicule of " Firmilian," however, though seemingly less harmless, could not be so well answered—first, from its very nature ; and, further, because unfortunately it was in a good measure deserved ;—and the felicitously conceived nickname of " Spasmodic" was a barbed arrow which, hitting, stuck. Smith bore this double attack with surprising equanimity and great fortitude, while it both injured him and did him good. Commercially, it marred the sale of his books, and so pecuniarily he suffered by it ; while, at the same time, it sobered his poetic genius, and purged it of the sins of his youth. His own spirit had, indeed, of itself begun to recoil against the spasmodic character of his first book, but the chastising hand of Aytoun confirmed his repentance. Nor was he the only one who profited by " Firmilian"—that, though an unmerciful, was a well-timed and most salutary satire, which laughed out of popular favour a very unwholesome kind of poetry which

had already received too much countenance, and
was corrupting the literature of our age and
country.   The rising generation of poets were
rapidly renouncing the simplicity of nature, and,
if not spasmodic, were at least too sensational.
Genius seemed too often intoxicated, or fevered,
rather than inspired.   The muse of song, forsaking
ordinary human life, endeavoured to lure us away
to a shadowy mist-magnifying land bordering on
the realms of spiritual existence, where men that
were not men, and women who were not women,
but male and female demi-gods, or semi-demons—
a mind-begotten hybrid race—now strutted rather
than walked the stage of life, mouthing "great
swelling words of vanity;" and anon endeavoured
to scale the heavens and talk with the celestials
familiarly as equals; or to dive into the abysmal
depths of the nether world, where their eyes lighted
up with an unusual kindly look.   The life
depicted in these poets' pages had neither the
dignity of tragedy nor the sprightliness of pan-
tomime; it often, however, partook more of the

nature of the latter than of the former ; was pan-
tomime with pantaloon and clown,—the most
human elements, after all, of that species of performance, left out. All the stars in the poetical
firmament were spirtively threatening to become
comets. To shine seemed nothing ; to glare was
grand. What matters might have come to under
these pigmy Miltons and Dantes it is hard to say,
had not Aytoun and others called them at length
to a more sober mood.

Unfortunately, however, "Firmilian" happened
to hit most heavily those who had transgressed
least—Gilfillan and Smith. Aytoun seemed to
reserve all his sharpest strokes for his own countrymen. Gilfillan, especially, was both most cruelly
and unjustly dealt with : while of Smith it might
be said that he was not only the youngest and
least guilty of the whole school, but the first,
besides, who himself saw his error and resolved to
abandon it. But treated as he was, he showed true
nobleness of character in entertaining at the time
no feelings of animosity towards his merciless

o

reprover. And it is very pleasant indeed to read in his essay on " Sydney Dobell," published among " Last Leaves," with how quiet and gentle a spirit he could, ten years afterwards, refer to "Firmilian" —its influence and its author ; while it is not less pleasant to know that Aytoun, not very long after he so unsparingly lashed the author of " A Life Drama," extended towards him a most generous, friendly hand, introducing him to the pages of " Blackwood," and that a cordial friend-ship existed between them till the one followed the other with an interval of only a few months to the quiet grave.

" City Poems," which appears to be presently out of print, has, if we mistake not, been gradually rising in public estimation, and is destined to rise still higher, and take the very first place among all Smith's poetical works. After its publication, he immediately devoted himself to the production of a historical poem, " Edwin of Deira." But mis-fortune still followed him ; for though he spent four years in its composition, Alfred Tennyson's

"Idylls of the King"—a kindred subject—appeared before its publication, and so rendered Smith again liable to the suspicion of imitation, besides bringing him into unfortunate comparison with the laureate. Not that there were any genuine or great grounds for such comparison, however, being made ; for the two works bear little or no resemblance to each other. Tennyson's is much the larger of the two poems, there is greater variety of character also in it, and he takes a firmer hold of his subject, and gives to it more depth and compactness ; but Smith's "Edwin" sparkles more with gems than the "Idylls" do. But there was only occasion for comparison in the sequence of the two works—nothing more. And, after all, the want of acceptance by the public in Smith's case, did not, perhaps, result so much from the publication of Tennyson's book at this time, as from the fact that public favour had meanwhile, for a season at least, left him as a poet. It is very questionable, indeed, if at this period of his career any poem published by Smith would

have met with a greater sale than "Edwin" did;
unless it had been a veritable "Paradise Lost."
The work is not without great intrinsic merits.   It
is by far the most classical in construction and
composition of all his poems.   It breathes also a
more healthy spirit than of any them.   But in the
literary as well as the physical world, when the
tide recedes a man must just patiently wait its
return.   It was, however, perhaps, so far unfortunate that "Edwin of Deira," notwithstanding
all its merits, was, for immediate wide acceptance
by the public, rather too unlike Mr. Smith's
previous poetical productions.   Those who had
admired his earlier volumes so highly, could not
all be expected to admire this one, in which the
most peculiar traits of his original genius had
almost entirely disappeared.   But, further, notwithstanding its great merits, it does not, on the
whole, equal "City Poems," in poetic value.   The
most valuable thing in "Edwin of Deira" was the
promise which it gave of what the author might
yet have done, in this, to him, new domain of

poesy, had years and leisure been allowed him. With such promise it was very rich indeed. That is an article in literature, however, which the general public have neither much discernment to perceive nor inclination to pay for. And it is still more to be regretted that neither his critics nor himself seemed to perceive this very clearly. So, as he neither gained pecuniarily, nor appeared to increase his fame by the publication of this book, he became, it is to be feared, a little dis-heartened—lost some measure of the passionate love for his harp which he once felt, and im-mediately turned his attention more to prose composition. "Edwin of Deira" was his last poetic production of any considerable length. He never abandoned poetry, however; nor could he do so,—

> "For it was his nature
> To blossom into song, as 'tis a tree's
> To leaf itself in April."

But his future poetical productions were confined to small pieces for the magazines, with the exception of a poem on "Edinburgh" which he had on hand, and which had only progressed a short way, when he died.

His chief prose work is "Dreamthorp," a volume of essays having few equals in the English language. In it he celebrates the praises of the country, as in his poems he had done those of the town. It is by this volume that he will live longest as an exquisite prose writer, and on it his fame in that department of literature will mainly depend. It gained for him the name of Essayist.

In 1865 he published, next, "A Summer in Skye," two volumes of very racy and graphic sketching of natural scenery and men and manners, which afford very pleasant reading. The work, however, is slightly marred in unity by extraneous matter at the beginning and close. These two parts constitute excrescences which it is desirable may be removed from future editions of this otherwise exquisite work.

In the same year also he edited an edition of

"Burns" for Macmillan, with a memoir and glossary; and continued, from month to month to supply "Good Words" with his only prose tale, entitled "Alfred Hagart's Household," which has since been published in a separate form in two volumes.

Numerous smaller articles from his pen had meantime graced the columns of several newspapers and the pages of sundry magazines and Encyclopedias. Some of the magazine articles have, since his death, been reprinted in the volume entitled "Last Leaves." These works greatly increased his literary reputation. As a prose writer, in fact, he had now become a great and growing favourite with the public, and as a genial and wise moralist he was rapidly rising to a first place among British essayists. But the work performed by him during the last two years had been too great for any man regularly occupied, as he was, in an office daily from ten o'clock a.m. till four o'clock p.m.; and consequently, he began to suffer from an over-wrought brain. Indeed, during the greater part of these two years he was labouring under such a malady, without knowing what ailed him, or taking the only means of cure for this distemper—entire mental rest. As evidence of this, it is very painful now to read such reflections as the following in the second volume of " A Summer in Skye " :—

"When I came up here a month or two ago, I was tired, jaded, ill at ease; I put spots in the sun, I flecked the loveliest blue of summer sky with bars of darkness; I felt the weight of the weary hours. Each morning called me as a slave-driver calls his slave. In sleep there was no refreshment; for in dream the weary day repeated itself yet more wearily. I was nervous, apprehensive of evil, irritable—ill in fact." (p. 214.) During all the following year, he continued more or less in this melancholy condition, and all the while was doing more mental work than previously. Surely none of his friends who knew this, but because he looked rosy all the while, " rather fleered at than sympathised with him," "thinking his complaint some form of mere hypochondria," had ever felt themselves the baneful effects of an exhausted brain. How one now wishes he had earlier told all to some experienced physician. For two years his holidays only tended to delay the fatal hour. It was a year of entire, and not two months of partial, rest he needed. At length the crisis came. And on November 20, 1866, he lay down upon his bed. His illness, which had now assumed the form of gastric fever, became complicated with diphtheria, and, after deceitful symptoms of recovery, lapsed into typhoid fever; so gradually sinking under the baneful influences of these malignant maladies, despite the skill of the best of the far-famed physicians of the Scottish capital, and the most assiduous care of those who loved him most, he breathed, at length, his last breath, in his house at Wardie, at nine o'clock on the morning of 5th, January, 1867, at the age of thirty-seven years and four days.

The news of his early death affected with unusual sorrow the whole literary and reading world. But still deeper far was he mourned by his relatives and numerous personal friends; for he had been a truly good, genial, generous, loving and most loveable man—such a friend as in this world is too rarely found, but once found can never be forgotten, and though lost by death must ever be missed and mourned.

On 10th January his body was borne to Warriston cemetery by sorrowing bereaved ones; and as they laid it there in the grave, "the cold but rich light of the early sunset seemed in melancholy harmony with the last scene of his bright and brief career;" but brief as, indeed, that career was, a sable company gathered again, about two months afterwards, around that grave, told of a briefer still, as they laid beside the father the remains of his first-born and much loved little daughter, of whose nativity he had sung most touchingly in his exquisite lyric of "Blaavin."

His last resting-place is now marked by a

memorial of loving hearts. In the beginning of
1868, was erected there a beautiful Runic cross
monument, with appropriate embellishments,
the design of which was furnished as a tribute
of affection by Mr. James Drummond, R.S.A.,
and containing a medallion likeness of the departed, which was executed by Mr. William
Brodie, sculptor, another friend. This monument
bears the simple inscription, "Alexander Smith,
Poet and Essayist. Erected by some of his
personal friends."

But, after all, his noblest monument is that
which he himself erected—his life. Seldom if
ever, indeed, has one so eminently gifted with a
poetic temperament and genius, manifested such
self-government, or lived a life so well balanced,
beautiful, and blameless. That life is the best
lesson he has taught us. It is a valuable legacy
to all, but especially to aspiring young men
and all candidates in literature. May many such
profit by it!

Butler and Tanner,
The Selwood Printing Works,
Frome, and London.